T0274951

Praise for the 2014 edition of *Gaza Writes Back*

The raw humanity, tenderness, and defiance in this collection of short stories by young Palestinians in Gaza stands as a testament to the resilience, moral fortitude, and beauty of oppressed and violated people everywhere. The writers are barely in their twenties and though their lives echo of bombs, bullets, and Israel's intentional programs to dismantle them, their stories teach us what it means to have an unconquered spirit and unbroken will. These are the next generation of Palestinian writers and intellectuals. We should all nurture their voices, lift them up, and read their stories then pass them on.

—SUSAN ABULHAWA
Author, *My Voice Sought the Wind* and *Mornings in Jenin*

What these stories provide, more than anything, is a human side to a conflict that remains largely faceless to the rest of the world. These stories are about parents and children, neighbors and friends, all of whom share a common tragedy.

Gaza Writes Back illustrates the power of the pen in offering a narrative that has otherwise been suppressed by decades of misinformation. It also takes a critical look within Palestinian society to highlight important issues.

In a land where hope is the most precious commodity passed down through the generations, these stories provide a tangible platform for silenced voices to be heard and means towards gaining some dignity for a wounded nation.

—RAMZY BAROUD
Author, *My Father Was a Freedom Fighter: Gaza's Untold Story*

These are stories that will give you for the first time the vivid texture of life and death as young Gazans felt them through Israel's Operation Cast Lead in 2008–9. These are intimate tales of devastation—sharp as a knife and unforgettable. Families, playmates, or the writers themselves, are maimed or killed in a flash by Israeli firepower, but this new generation is writing as a form of resistance.

Here are poignant echoes of the stories of Ghassan Kanafani. (He was assassinated in Beirut in 1972, but his stories have never died.) Forty years on these new stories of children's dreams and deaths are being written by nearly two dozen Kanafanis. The book's skillful editor sets the context with a brilliant opening quotation from the great Nigerian writer Chinua Achebe: "Storytellers are a threat....they frighten usurpers of the right-to-freedom of the human spirit."

—VICTORIA BRITTAIN
Author, *Shadow Lives: The Forgotten Women of the War on Terror*

This collection of marvelous first-hand stories expresses as only good literature can the feel of life and death in Gaza. Here are moving, poignant snapshots of real experience which will haunt and fascinate the reader with their eloquence. It is time that Gazans spoke out against their dehumanization and the world heard them. Essential reading to understand what has been done to Gaza and how its brave people remain unbowed.

—Dr. GHADA KARMI
Author, *In Search of Fatima: A Palestinian Story*

This volume of short stories marks the fifth anniversary of the infamous 2008–9 Israeli attack on Gaza, "Operation Cast Lead." Our familiarity with what happened then does not lessen the power of the cruel lines etched into their writers' memories, nor disguise their need to write and thus master the terrible realities of Palestinian life.

For anyone who values the raw voice of human experience over the rarefied refinements of professional writing, these short stories will come as a shock. Instead of the sanitized and heartless statistics of the toll taken by those weeks, or the impersonal photographs and official reports that record the brutal attack and the occupation, we have lightly fictionalized intimate, personal accounts of the lived experiences. Though death, illness and horrific violence stalk every page, the stories and their writers shine through as strong, truthful, and sometimes even cheerful or romantic. Always, however, they clearly represent an unspoken determination to resist the violence, and a brave resolve not to surrender to despair.

—JEAN SAID MAKDISI
Author, *Beirut Fragments: A War Memoir*

Gaza Writes Back...takes us up close and personal into the minds of a young articulate Palestinian generation born stateless, under occupation, and growing into adulthood under siege in one of the world's most oppressed and dangerous environments.

This is a generation that is physically confined within Israel's walls and emotionally scarred by Israel's relentless bombings and incursions.... This book expresses anger at the uncertainty of life while the writers continue to cling to faith and hope....

The overwhelming voices of young female writers and their refined eloquence and capacity to express dissent not only challenge our stereotypical perception of Palestinians and women in Gaza in particular, but they also challenge the norms within Palestinian society itself....

This book is a promise of a change in societal norms and a positive sign of what is to come. Despite the horror, the frustration, the physical and emotional scars, the voices in *Gaza Writes Back* have not given up on their ambitions and have not resigned their dreams for a better future.

—SAMAH SABAWI
Palestinian writer, originally from Gaza

GAZA WRITES BACK

GAZA WRITES BACK

Short Stories from Young Writers in Gaza, Palestine

Memorial Edition

Refaat Alareer, PhD, Editor

Just World Books
WASHINGTON, D.C.

Just World Books
Timely Books for Changing Times

Just World Books, LLC.

Front cover design by Just World Books
Typesetting by Diana Ghazzawi

ISBN: 9781682571019 (print) 9781682571026 (ebook)

Cataloging-in-Publication data is available from the Library of Congress.

Contents

Foreword by Ali Abunimah   11

To Palestine, To Gaza by Refaat Alareer   19

Editor's Introduction   21

Note About Some of the Words Used   33

The Stories   35

    L for Life by Hanan Habashi   37

    One War Day by Mohammed Suliman   45

    Spared by Rawan Yaghi   51

    Canary by Nour Al-Sousi   55

    The Story of the Land by Sarah Ali   61

    Toothache in Gaza by Samiha Olwan   67

    Will I Ever Get Out? by Nour Al-Sousi   73

    A Wall by Rawan Yaghi   77

    A Wish for Insomnia by Nour El Borno   79

    Bundles by Mohammed Suliman   83

On a Drop of Rain by Refaat Alareer   **89**

Please Shoot to Kill by Jehan Alfarra   **91**

Omar X by Yousef Aljamal   **103**

We Shall Return by Mohammed Suliman   **107**

From Beneath by Rawan Yaghi   **113**

Just Fifteen Minutes by Wafaa Abu Al-Qomboz   **115**

House by Refaat Alareer   **119**

Neverland by Tasnim Hamouda   **129**

Lost at Once by Elham Hilles   **131**

It's My Loaf of Bread by Tasnim Hamouda   **141**

Once Upon a Dawn by Shahd Awadallah   **143**

The Old Man and the Stone by Refaat Alareer   **151**

Scars by Aya Rabah   **155**

About the Writers   **165**

Acknowledgments   **207**

Foreword

by Ali Abunimah

"REFAAT, ANY NEWS?"

That was my last WhatsApp message, on December 5, 2023, to the editor of this book. I hadn't heard from him for two days, when we had a brief but worrying exchange of messages. "The attacks have not stopped. Just now, tens of bombs," Refaat wrote from Gaza City. "My heart is in my socks. I am horrified."

A week earlier, on November 30, Refaat had made an appearance on the *Electronic Intifada*'s livestream. We launched the regular program on YouTube soon after the events of October 7, as a place to share news, analysis, comfort, and grief, and to provide a platform for people in Gaza to bear witness to what they were experiencing. It was the last day of a week-long truce and prisoner exchange between the Palestinian resistance and the Israelis that many hoped would turn into a permanent ceasefire.

"I haven't seen my kids since the truce started," a gaunt-looking Refaat said, his beard fuller than usual, as he sat in the office he'd arranged to use for the interview. "They moved to another place, and I am spending most of the time running to places with internet connections so I can be online," he explained. "I'm not sure how this is going to end, but with what we have now, it's complete and utter destruction," Refaat added, his voice subdued. "I keep citing World War II as a reference. The destruction we see in pictures is happening right in front of our eyes."

As soon as he spoke those words, the lights blinked off and Refaat's face froze, dimly lit for a split second only by the screen of the laptop he had been speaking to us through. And then he disappeared. We'd been able to speak to him for just four minutes.

On the following week's livestream, I reassured the audience—and myself—that although we hadn't been able to reach Refaat for days, this was undoubtedly due to the lack of electricity and connectivity in Gaza. The truce had ended and Israel's savage and indiscriminate bombardment had resumed. I still felt sure that before long, Refaat's name would pop up in my notifications with one of his jokes or his typical response, "We are fine"—words I took only to mean "We are alive."

No one in Gaza is fine.

But that reassurance was not to be. Moments after we ended the program, I received a message from a mutual friend: "Ali, Refaat is dead."

Now, almost seven months later, the meaning of those words has yet to sink in. Part of me still waits for Refaat to respond to my last message.

What we know is that on December 6, 2023, Refaat was at the home of his sister Asmaa in the al-Sidra neighborhood of Gaza City. At about 6 pm, Israeli forces fired a missile at the building killing Refaat, his brother Salah and one of Salah's sons, and Asmaa and three of her children. Refaat, the father of six children, was just 44 years old.

The airstrike surgically targeted the apartment on the second floor, not the whole building—a clear indication that the apartment, and almost certainly Refaat himself, was the intended target. His killing was part of Israel's systematic and targeted extermination of Gaza's leading intellectuals, academics, and scientists—a hallmark of genocide. By late January 2024, Israel had murdered at least 94 university professors, along with hundreds of teachers and thousands of students. It had destroyed every university in Gaza and damaged or destroyed hundreds of schools.

The scale of the genocide in Gaza reverberates through this book, even though it was first published more than a decade earlier. This new edition contains short About the Writers essays from nine of the original storytellers. But the publishers were unable to contact the other story contributors in time to get their updated self-descriptions into this edition, and the fate of several of them remains unknown.

A friend of Refaat told the Euro-Med Human Rights Monitor that days before he was murdered, Refaat had received an anonymous call from someone who identified himself as an Israeli officer. The caller warned Refaat that they knew precisely which school he was sheltering in and that advancing Israeli ground forces would soon reach his location. That call prompted Refaat to move to his sister's apartment, likely thinking it was less conspicuous than the overcrowded school, where his continued presence could endanger many more people if Israel sought to kill him.

This was Refaat. He always put others first. Just a few weeks earlier, Refaat and his family had been sheltering at the Al-Rantisi children's hospital in Gaza City. They fled there after Israel bombed their apartment building in Tal al-Hawa. But the hospital would not provide safety for long.

"On November 10, my daughter Shymaa woke me up and showed me a video of the Israeli tanks right below our window," Refaat recalled in his last article for the *Electronic Intifada*. "It was terrifying. The tank was huge."

As Israeli forces gathered to attack and occupy the hospital—which they would do the following day, claiming falsely that Israeli captives were held there by Hamas—Refaat understood the urgency of leaving. He gathered about two dozen people together, mostly children.

"Listen," he said. "I do not want anyone to cry and scream. I will be blunt." He laid out the frightening scenario the group could face from the Israeli soldiers as they tried to leave the besieged hospital: "They might let the women and children go and shoot the young men."

"That point elicited a number of screams," Refaat wrote. But he was firm. "If that is the case, and I want to be clear, do not look back," he instructed. "No matter what happens to us. Do not scream or cry. Keep going east. Keep running."

Terrifying though it was, they survived that day. And as Refaat observed, the fact that Israel allowed everyone to leave proved that its claims of Hamas activities at the hospital were lies. No one was detained or even questioned.

Refaat's friend Asem al-Nabih, a member of the Gaza City municipality's emergency committee, was one of the last people to see him alive. "Over the past days and weeks, he and I would walk every day. He always looked everywhere for inspiration. He looked at everything," Asem recalled after Refaat's murder.

"Anyone who knew Refaat, knows that he was a very solid man. Steadfast in unimaginable ways," Asem said. But the day before he was killed, Refaat surprised Asem by admitting how exhausted he was.

"I'm tired of carrying water. I'm tired. I am responsible for 50 people," Asem recalled Refaat saying. Refaat continued to walk around his beloved Gaza City with Asem, searching for eSIM cards or a mobile phone signal.

"You would find him climbing on top of high walls, lifting his arm up to get reception, putting himself in danger, just to convey a message." Though he was tired, Refaat never stopped caring for others. "When he walked down the streets, he would advise random people, telling them where to go, where to be safe," Asem said.

The last thing Refaat told him, according to Asem, was that "If God kept him alive, he would want to focus all his life to tell the stories of his people and their experiences and feelings."

The truth is that Refaat had already devoted his life to this mission—as this book, first published in 2014, attests. In his Editor's Introduction, Refaat explains—far more eloquently than I can—the power of stories to break mental and physical bonds, to reshape perceptions and thus be a tool to create a new, more just world. When I re-read it today, it is as fresh, poignant, and relevant as on the day Refaat wrote it.

And throughout the genocide, until his murder, Refaat never stopped doing the work he loved. Despite the desperate struggle to find water, food, and safety, he would message me whenever he could, forwarding drafts of articles written by his students scattered across a burning Gaza. He would help, encourage, and sometimes admonish them to write stories, poems, and testimonies, and send them to us at the *Electronic Intifada* to share with the world. And we did.

"All those pieces you publish for my students keep me going," he wrote me less than a month into the genocide.

Refaat's dedication to Gaza and its people reflected his own deep love for a place long abandoned by the world. He believed in Gaza. Following his graduate studies in the UK and earning a PhD in Malaysia, Refaat, who could have gone anywhere, went back to Gaza, determined to serve his community. He became a professor of English literature at the Islamic University of Gaza, the institution where he had done his undergraduate studies. He had chosen to major in English literature, and as an educator he imparted his love for poetry and the plays of Shakespeare to generations of students.

The proud son of a laborer, and the second of 14 children, Refaat was a child of Shujaiya, the Gaza City district whose name means "land of the brave." Like so many Palestinians, Refaat's earliest memories were marred by Israeli violence. While he was a child, his father and mother were nearly killed on separate occasions by Israeli bullets and shells. He himself was shot by Israeli soldiers with rubber-coated steel bullets, and on one occasion, an Israeli soldier threw a rock at him from the roof of a building, injuring him in the head.

Even before the genocide, Refaat and his wife Nusayba had between them lost dozens of relatives to Israel's decades of occupation and persecution of the Palestinian people. During its onslaught against Gaza in the summer of 2014, Israel bombed the home of Nusayba's sister, killing her and her husband and several of the couple's children. This horrifying toll, Refaat wrote in a May 2021 op-ed for the *New York Times*, made them "a perfectly average Palestinian couple."

The first piece Refaat ever wrote for the *Electronic Intifada*, in 2014, told the story of his martyred brother Mohamed—Hamada—who was beloved by children across Gaza, Palestine, and the Arab world for his character Karkour, a mischievous chicken he played on TV.

Israel destroyed Refaat's home during the 2014 war, a building that housed dozens of members of his extended family. Asem recalls accompanying his friend to the ruins, where Refaat went straight to the room where he kept all his students' poems and stories.

"They were all burned and scattered on the floor, and he would pick through the rubble to salvage what he could as if he was gathering treasure," Asem remembered. "To him these stories and poems were the most precious memories of his beloved students."

When Refaat's building was destroyed by Israel in October 2023, he lamented in a text message the loss of the "thousands of books I collected over 30 years."

"The books can be replaced, Refaat. You cannot," I responded. "You have at least another 30 years ahead of you to collect books. Maybe 50 years."

He barely had another 30 days. And thanks to Israel, Refaat's losses would not end after his death. On April 26, 2024, Israel murdered Refaat's beloved daughter Shymaa, along with her husband Muhammad Abd al-Aziz Siyam and their infant son Abd al-Rahman, in what appeared to be another deliberately targeted surgical strike. Shortly after Abd al-Rahman was born, Shymaa had posted a message on social media, addressed to her deceased father. "I have beautiful news for you, and I wish I could tell you while you were in front of me, handing you your first grandchild. Did you know that you have become a grandfather?" Shymaa wrote.

Ahmed Nehad, a close friend and colleague of Refaat, noted that Refaat's now world-famous 2011 poem, "If I Must Die," was actually written for Shymaa. "She's the one that was told to tell his story, to sell his things, and to not lose hope," Ahmed said.

In an interview with Al Jazeera some years ago, Refaat described how Shymaa—then just 5 years old—inspired him to start telling stories during Israel's first major war on Gaza in December 2008–January 2009. "During the first war on Gaza, the most painful thing was the horror the children went through," Refaat said. Stories were a way to enthrall and distract them, to escape to a world of imagination beyond the confines of an otherwise inescapable reality. Refaat soon discovered their greater power.

Most of the stories Refaat wrote, and encouraged his students to write and publish, are nonfiction, ranging from very personal narratives to traditional journalistic reporting. Refaat celebrated every sort of writing and storytelling, especially his famously astute, witty, and fearless posts on social media. But Refaat saw *Gaza Writes Back*, a collection of fictional short stories, as a radical experiment in the context of Gaza, taking his mission to another level. He explains in his Editor's Introduction that unlike journalistic writing or op-eds, "fiction, with its humanist concern and universal appeal, goes further, by touching many more people, and does so not just momentarily but for many decades into the future."

Refaat co-founded We Are Not Numbers, a project launched in Gaza after Israel's 2014 attack, to mentor and support young writers in the besieged territory to tell their stories to the world in English. It was and remains a spectacular success. It is through We Are Not Numbers that the publication I edit, the *Electronic Intifada*, has been introduced to many of its writers in and from Gaza. They, like Refaat, have insisted on continuing to write, especially during the genocide.

Refaat had a profound impact on thousands of students in Gaza. He had a rare ability to make each and every person he spoke to feel that they were the only person in the world who mattered to him, and to encourage them to push themselves beyond their own boundaries. His murder set off an outpouring of grief and outrage around the world, even among those who had not yet encountered his work, let alone had the chance to meet him in person.

I treasure the memories of the times I spent with Refaat in Washington, DC, Philadelphia, Chicago, and California when he came to the United States in 2014, with contributors Yousef Aljamal and Rawan Yaghi, to promote *Gaza Writes Back*. I feel his absence acutely but with each passing day I appreciate ever more the impact he had on me and on the world.

When Refaat's beloved brother Hamada was killed in 2014, Refaat wrote, "Israel's barbarity to murder people in Gaza and to sever the connections between people and people, and between people and land and between people and memories, will never succeed."

"I lost my brother physically, but the connection with him will remain forever and ever," Refaat added.

He taught us that stories are what bind us together and keep our hope alive.

Refaat too is still with us, through his own words, and the words of the many young Palestinians he continues to inspire to write their own stories and the stories of their people.

~June 2024

To Palestine, To Gaza

by Refaat Alareer

And despite Israel's death sentences
Like lead
Cast upon the head,
Gnawing at our life,
Clinging to it like a flea to a kitten,
And stuffed in our throats
The moment we say "Amen"
To the prayers of old women and men
Blocking their ways to God,
We dream and pray,
Clinging to life even harder
Every time a dear one's life
Is forcibly rooted up.
We live. We live.
We do.

Editor's Introduction

Storytellers are a threat. They threaten all champions of
control, they frighten usurpers of the right-to-freedom of the
human spirit....

—Chinua Achebe,
in *Anthills of the Savannah*

SOMETIMES A HOMELAND BECOMES A TALE. WE LOVE THE STORY
because it is about our homeland, and we love our homeland
even more because of the story.

This is the first book of its kind. *Gaza Writes Back* re-
cords and commemorates, in fiction, the fifth anniversary of
the full-scale military offensive Israel launched on Gaza between December 27, 2008 and January 18, 2009, the so-called
"Operation Cast Lead." Written by young writers from Gaza,
the stories included here present, in English, a much-needed
Palestinian youth narrative without the mediation or influences
of translation or of non-Palestinian voices. *Gaza Writes Back*
comes to resist Israel's attempts to murder these emerging voices, to squander the suffering of the martyrs, to bleach the blood,
to dam the tears, and to smother the screams. This book shows
the world that despite Israel's continuous attempts to kill steadfastness in us, Palestinians keep going on, never surrendering to
pain or death, and always seeing and seeking liberty and hope
in the darkest of times. *Gaza Writes Back* provides conclusive
evidence that telling stories is an act of life, that telling stories is resistance, and that telling stories shapes our memories.

Samiha Olwan, a contributor to this book, noted in particular that, "Cyberspace, as a newly centralized space in which the act of storytelling is constantly in process, provides scattered Palestinians with a place which holds new possibilities of forging new ways of belonging or place-making."

Stories and narratives, part of every human gathering, enable people to make sense of their past and relate it to their present; they can be the main thread attaching them to their past, and they can present the form of a dream yet to be fulfilled. Palestinians in particular have grown to cherish, and to seek, stories. Indeed, storytelling is itself a major theme of some of the stories in this book, because the writers know well that stories outlive every other human experience. No family gathering ever lacks one or more stories of those good old days when Palestine was the Palestine that current generations have not known or experienced directly. And since everyone has been subjected to stories and storytelling, there is a Palestine that dwells inside all of us, a Palestine that needs to be rescued: a free Palestine where all people regardless of color, religion, or race coexist; a Palestine where the meaning of the word "occupation" is only restricted to what the dictionary says rather than those plenty of meanings and connotations of death, destruction, pain, suffering, deprivation, isolation, and restrictions that Israel has injected the word with. These horrendous Israeli practices and many others, Palestinian writers—particularly the young ones—capture and materialize in the form of narratives in an attempt to make sense of the senseless context around them and in search of their Palestine. Theirs, while it sometimes is rendered metaphorically, can be a beautiful reality. Palestine is a martyr away, a tear away, a missile away, or a whimper away. Palestine is a story away.

Operation Cast Lead

Operation Cast Lead was deeply traumatic for all of us who were in Gaza at the time. But looked at in perspective it was only one in a series of very deadly assaults that the Israeli military, and before 1948 the Jewish militias in Palestine, have launched against Palestine's indigenous population. In the fighting of 1947–48, the Jewish and Israeli forces assailed Palestinian villages and towns both inside and far beyond the borders that the United Nations had "given" to the Jewish state, and they drove out as many Palestinians as they could from the areas they brought under Israel's control. In 1956, Israel invaded Gaza and all of Egypt's Sinai Peninsula, visiting many terrible massacres on the people of Gaza. In 1967, Israel invaded Gaza again, and also the whole of the West Bank including East Jerusalem. It held these areas under the temporary situation that international lawyers call "foreign military occupation"; forty-five years later, it still holds them, controlling the populations of both areas under the iron grip of military law. In the West Bank, the Israeli authorities have implanted more than 600,000 Israeli civilian settlers into the area in direct defiance of international law. Around Gaza, it has maintained a tight siege, punctuated by eruptions of savage and deadly violence. For many years, Israel's well-armed military battled Palestinian freedom fighters and sowed terror in Palestinian refugee communities in Lebanon. Its secret services have assassinated Palestinian intellectuals and suspected leaders in Beirut, Tunis, Norway, Malta, Dubai—and many times in the West Bank and Gaza....

Even when viewed through the lens of this history, the impacts of Israel's Cast Lead assault on Gaza were far-reaching. The death and destruction that Israel indiscriminately flung upon the heads of the Gazan people caused more than 1,400 deaths, more than 5,000 injuries, and the destruction or severe damage of more than 11,000 homes and innumerable industrial buildings, shops, roads, bridges, and other infrastructure. The sudden deaths and bombing, and the first scenes of the torn bodies of scores of police cadets, left scars in the souls and hearts of all Palestinians and of free people around the world, as social media outlets allowed for the first time minute-by-minute coverage. More and more people around the globe started mobilizing for Gaza. And more and more people started writing. The strikes that claimed the lives of hundreds of police cadets, school children, and civilians also kindled a grand passion among many Palestinians, especially in Gaza, for writing. During the offensive, Palestinians in Gaza realized more than ever before that no one, no matter who and no matter where, is immune from Israel's fire. Israel cast lead indiscriminately hither and thither, aiming to melt not just our bodies, which it did, but also our allegiance and our hope and our memories, which it could not do. Twenty-three days later, the people of Gaza rose to dust themselves off and to start an arduous journey of rebuilding houses and infrastructure, and reconstructing what the missiles had dispersed and scattered. Twenty-three days of nonstop Israeli hate and hostility—and Gaza rose from it like a phoenix.

The people who queued at the morgues and bade farewell to their loved ones days later queued at bakeries that did not raise their prices, and went out to the grocery stores that also did not raise their prices. And they came back home to distribute what little they bought to the people who were unable to buy because they did not have the money. The people of Gaza were never this close before. Gaza was now more deeply rooted not only in the hearts of every Palestinian, but also in the hearts of every free soul around the globe. Gaza stood head and shoulders above all else. Gaza never stooped. Gaza taught us to fight oppression with what little we have, by any means necessary. Gaza taught us never to kneel, and not even to think of it. That is why we produced this book: to honor this feature in Gaza. But this is not to romanticize war. War is by all means ugly. "There was too much pain in those twenty-three days, and some of us who wrote about Cast Lead, did so to heal some of the pain caused by the horrendous memories. And no matter how beautiful the spirit of resistance that overwhelmed us, this beauty should never override the ugliness of pure injustice," as Samiha Olwan put it.

Many swore to fight back, many others swore to cover their backs, and some Gazans took to their pens, or their keyboards. They swore to expose Israel's aggressiveness and write, in English, so that the whole world could get to know the so-called "only democracy" in the Middle East, that two years before 2008 had, with the help of the Western powers, smothered a newly born democracy in Palestine. These bloggers and activists are the ones who made this book a reality. And like any society, Palestine is not perfect, something the stories touch upon. In addition to addressing occupation issues, the stories also have social purposes, as they never fail to point the finger of accusations, usually symbolically, at aging Palestinian leadership and certain undesired social conventions.

This is not to suggest that Palestinian fiction writing by emerging young writers is reactive; it's rather a very creative, proactive response: to resist in words the horrible situations imposed upon them. The time was ripe for this wave of writers to emerge. They have the tools—an excellent command of English and social media skills—the motivation, the enthusiasm, and most importantly the understanding that "writing back" to Israel's long occupation, constant aggressiveness, and Operation Cast Lead is a moral obligation and a duty they are paying back to Palestine and to a bleeding, yet resilient, Gaza. In addition, writing back is an act of resistance and an obligation to humanity to spread the words to the whole world and to raise awareness among people blinded by multi-million-dollar Israeli campaigns of *hasbara* ("persuasion," or more accurately, disinformation.)

The Stories and the Writers

The twenty-three stories in this volume were chosen from tens of submissions. All were originally written in English, except "Canary" and "Will I Ever Get Out?" (which were translated by Refaat Alareer and Mohammed Suliman, respectively). The stories were written by fifteen writers, only three of whom are male. Almost half of the stories started out as class assignments in my Creative Writing or Fiction classes. Many of the writers started as bloggers, and many had never written fiction before. Working closely with many young talents in Gaza has proven to me that all they need is proper encouragement, practical training, and close attention in order to blossom.

These stories present the unmediated voices of young people who are fed up with the occupation, the international community, and the aging Palestinian leadership. Embedded in these stories are rich layers of discourse and worldviews. Such worldviews sometimes echo old narratives or certain parts of them, but mostly they are unique, not merely in using English as a medium but also in giving profound insights into the Palestinian plight. As they wrote their stories, these writers were experimenting in many ways and at many different levels, starting with point of view, style, plot, and form. Particularly striking here are the stories that try to "invade" the psyches of Israeli soldiers, a relatively new phenomenon in the narratives of young people.

Even prior to Operation Cast Lead, young Palestinians were using blogging and social media to resist and expose the Israeli occupation. But the aftermath of the war witnessed a new influx of writers using these tools. Young people who had a very good command of English believed they had a chance to give voice to their worldviews. Many became very excited by the possibilities that their command of English and their social media skills gave them to break the isolation that Israel was constantly seeking to impose on them, and to connect with the solidarity activists from around the world who, in the years after Cast Lead, founded a plethora of new grassroots organizations to press for the rights of Palestinians—including the right of Gaza's Palestinians to be able to live a decent, normal life, free from the endless privations of the Israeli blockade.

Many of these writers have English as their university major, which means they read both English and world literature. They are also very well read in Palestinian writings of all genres. They have always sought inspiration from Edward Said, Ghassan Kanafani, Mahmoud Darwish, Jabra Ibrahim Jabra, Suad Amiry, Susan Abulhawa, Mourid and Tamim al-Barghouti, Ibrahim Nasrallah, Samah Sabawi, Ali Abunimah, these and many others. Writers like these clearly had an undeniable impact on the writings of the young Palestinian bloggers and writers. Therefore, writing that first started with a status on Facebook, a tweet on Twitter, a short blog post, and then long blog posts, evolved by practice and training into fiction writing, a genre that is more universal than any other type. The first wave of writing was mainly descriptive, a what-happened-and-what-I-think form of writing. That later gave way to fiction writing, which is the topic of this anthology. The move from writing articles, which some of those short story writers have done and still do, to writing fiction is a smart one. Opinion pieces and articles, while undeniably significant, usually have only short-lived impact and they tend to address people who already support you. But fiction, with its humanist concern and universal appeal, goes further by touching many more people, and does so not just momentarily but for many decades into the future. The young writers of this book well understand that fiction transcends time, belief, and place.

The book, as noted above, includes more female writers than male writers. The young women are not included at the expense of young men but because the fact on the ground is that more young female writers in Gaza use social media and write literature, particularly in English, than do their male counterparts. This shows how important young Palestinian women have become in recent years. They have managed to use all the available tools to take the initiative and play a significant role in preserving the Palestinian identity, resisting the occupation, and building a more open Palestinian society in which women and men are equal. The roles that Palestinian women have played throughout history are undeniable. And this young wave of female short story writers comes to continue the struggle and at the same time revolutionize it, adding their own sensibility and their own worldview. It is also notable that the women portrayed in the stories are powerful, independent, intellectual, and proactive. Their role is no longer restricted to giving birth to freedom fighters; they are the freedom fighters. How similar or dissimilar they are and what major concerns these young women voice in their stories should be left to researchers, academics, and reviewers to discuss.

Those young female writers who started as bloggers believed it was time to have their say and to contribute to standing by their people against the cruelty of the occupation by any means available. For the first time in the Palestinian struggle for independence, the young women take the lead in this form of resistance as female writers outnumbered male writers and, adopting the general framework of the existing Palestinian narratives, promote female issues and voice solutions and worldviews as powerful as those voiced by male writers. New narratives and voices, therefore, seem to have emerged, defying all the attempts to block them. In other words, the way in which Palestinian young women write—the language of their narrative/s, or the way a text is expressed—is a fight to prove the self. That is to say, it needs to be read with notions of identity—in this case notions of gender identity—in mind if it is to be fully understood.

The stories included in this volume are diverse in their themes, settings, forms, types, and experimentations. Although the book attempts to trace and record how young writers of the Gaza Strip reacted to Israel's 2008–9 military assault, the stories include Palestine as a whole as an attempt to refuse any kind of division. Among Palestinians, no matter where they are, there is an emphasis on the Right of Return. Some stories are about West Bank issues such as the Separation Wall, settlements, or Jerusalem. Some do not have a particular setting, to suggest that the story could happen anywhere in occupied Palestine, or even any people under occupation.

The stories range from simple, punchy pieces, to long and complex ones, from allegorical to child-like bedtime stories. This is a fascinating collection of stories that goes beyond purely literary values to unite and bring together the whole of Palestine in one narrative: while Gaza has to endure Israel's medieval siege and successive military assaults, the West Bank and Jerusalem have to experience Israel's Wall and checkpoints, Palestinians of 1948 have to suffer Israel's apartheid, and those in the Diaspora have to endure not being able to simply book a ticket and come back home any time they feel like it. Most if not all the Gaza writers in this book have never been to other places in Palestine. The internet was the place where they managed to meet and interact with Palestinians from the Diaspora, the West Bank, Jerusalem, and territories occupied in 1948. Together they piece and construct the territorial fragments of Palestine into a fascinating entity that Israel still refuses to allow to exist in reality. In fact, they wrote about things they never experienced, like the Wall, the checkpoints, and the settlements. *Gaza Writes Back* focuses on writers from Gaza; however, the book fights and refutes the common misunderstanding that Gaza is a separate entity.

Themes

The stories in this collection explore a number of issues, but key among them are the issues of land, of death and dying, and of memory.

Regarding land, Edward Said has written (in *Culture and Imperialism*):

> The main battle in imperialism is over land, of course; but when it came to who owned the land, who had the right to settle and work on it, who kept it going, who won it back, and who now plans the future—these issues were reflected, contested, even for a time decided in narrative.

A sense of the land develops from the spontaneous root-edness when one's relation to the land is threatened by others. The stories here are endowed with the passion with which Palestinians relate themselves to the land. Land, place, and trees are central motifs in the stories of *Gaza Writes Back*. This attachment to the land and soil continues to grow in spite of all the practices and measures Israel takes to detach Palestinians from their land. The harder Israel tries, the more attached to the land these people grow. Therefore, many of these stories can be read in the context of contesting the Israeli narrative and myths of ownership of Palestine.

Some readers may say death and dying permeate these stories. It is an undeniable feature of many of them. What else do we expect from a generation that spent a considerable part of its life looking death in the eye? Due to the occupation, death has become a daily encounter for most Palestinians. Still, beneath this layer lies an insistence on life and a determination to live. Between the lines of these stories is a desire for survival. The very act of writing tells of the hope of a better life the writers have. The desire to describe and explore the experiences of life—including, in this case, that of death—so that others might lead a better life is the very act of *sumud* or steadfastness that has long characterized Palestinian life. The notion of giving up, of surrendering to the occupation, to most Palestinians sounds quite repulsive.

With respect to memory, we should keep in mind that to tell a story is to remember and to help others remember. Many, if not all, of the stories here zoom in on minute details in an attempt to engrave such atrocities or such rare moments of hope into the writers' own memories and those of others. Because memories shape much of our world, telling these memories in the form of stories is an act of resistance to an occupation that works hard to obliterate and destroy links between Palestine and Palestinians. The stories here promote remembering and condemn forgetting. Even when the character is dying, his/her ultimate wish is for others to "to tell [the] story," as Hamlet put it. And telling the story thereby itself becomes an act of life. Further, some of the stories here even chase the Israeli soldiers into their own memories and consciences, declaring that there will be no rest for the occupiers and that we Palestinians will keep breathing down your necks until you realize that occupation needs to end, or else we will spoil your most intimate moments by yelling at the top of our lungs, "Enough! Enough!"

Living and Writing in Gaza Today

These stories were all, of course, composed under very harsh circumstances. Gaza has been under an Israeli siege since 2006. The Israeli military authorities eased the siege just a little in the period after their quite unjustified attack on the Freedom Flotilla in 2010, and then again just after the Arab Spring. (But after the disgraceful developments in Egypt in the summer of 2013, the noose around Gaza was pulled very tight once again.) The lengthy political, economic, and intellectual siege that Israel has maintained around Gaza meant that, as they worked on their stories, all of our writers—like every single person living in Gaza—had to cope with the constant and debilitating structural violence of power cuts, isolation, unemployment, lack of basic goods, lack of books, lack of medicine and access to health care, extreme difficulty in traveling outside Gaza, and far too often pain, death, or the loss of loved ones. Meanwhile, Israel never halted its constant, intrusive surveillance over Gaza or its frequent use of direct lethal violence against the area's 1.7 million people.

But the fiercer Israel grew, the more reasons Gaza's Palestinians found to live, and to stay. With endless resourcefulness and commitment, they found workarounds to the many problems the occupation created. Books, basic goods, fuel, building materials, and many other things were smuggled through tunnels. (Even brides came and went out of Gaza through tunnels, and a number, albeit pitifully small, of Palestinian refugees from Syria were able to flee the terrible situation there and find some shelter in Gaza.) Nothing could stop us from living. Instead, these writers and I made use of the terrible circumstances and explored them in our stories, in what might be described as counterattack narratives. These stories were born in circumstances of fear and uncertainty similar to those that poor Anne Frank had to suffer; we lived situations as bad as those we saw in the movie *The Pianist*. And like Anne Frank and those who resisted in *The Pianist*, like any people anywhere who have come under occupation, we resisted and insisted on fighting back. In our case, we have done so by writing.

In 2011, one part of the outpouring of global solidarity activism mentioned above was the project that a group of US citizens launched, to fill a whole boat with letters written to the people of Gaza by people from around the world who cared about their fate, and then to sail it in to Gaza's sea-lapped shore. They named their boat after the title of a book written (before his election) by President Barack Obama: *The Audacity of Hope*. Long before the boat could reach Gaza, the government of Greece, under great pressure from Israel, moved in and stopped it from completing its mission. But the spirit in which our book has been created and published is a spirit of strong reciprocity and appreciation for all the efforts made by people outside Gaza (including many very caring and well-known writers), to break through the intense intellectual and personal isolation in which Israel has sought to keep us caged. So now, five years after Operation Cast Lead, we are pleased to be able to tell everyone around the world who supports our right to live normal, and normally productive lives, that "Gaza Writes Back."

Gaza writes back because storytelling helps construct Palestinian national identity and unity. Gaza writes back because there is a Palestine that needs to be rescued, at least textually for the time being. Gaza tells stories because Palestine is at a short story's span. Gaza narrates so that people might not forget. Gaza writes back because the power of imagination is a creative way to construct a new reality. Gaza writes back because writing is a nationalist obligation, a duty to humanity, and a moral responsibility.

—Refaat Alareer
November 2013

Note About Some of the Words Used

There are a handful of terms in *Gaza Writes Back* which may be unfamiliar to the reader.

It is customary for men and women to be given an honorific name as the father or mother of their oldest son, *Abu* meaning "father of" and *Um* meaning "mother of." Thus, a couple who have a son named Samer may be called Abu Samer and Um Samer by family, friends, and acquaintances. Less commonly, someone may be named after his or her oldest daughter if he or she doesn't have a son, or the moniker may be given even if a person doesn't have a child. Palestinian children may use various names to address their parents. In this book, you'll find *Mama* and *Baba*, the equivalent of "Mom" and "Dad."

Kufiya is the traditional, checkered cloth worn as a scarf or headdress in Palestine and other Arab countries, where it may be known by other names.

'Eid is the Arabic word for "holiday." *'Eidiyya* is a holiday gift, usually money given to children.

The *shahada* is the Muslim declaration of faith.

The Nakba, meaning "catastrophe," is what Palestinians call their forced expulsion from their homeland as a result of the declaration of the state of Israel in 1948 and the seizure of Palestinian lands.

UNRWA is the United Nations Relief and Works Agency, the United Nations body established after 1948 to provide relief to the Palestinian refugees from that year on a temporary basis until they could return to their homes.

The Stories

L for Life

by Hanan Habashi

HOW ARE YOU, BABA? IT'S BEEN AGES SINCE I LAST SAT AND talked to you. I nearly forgot about my promise to write to you whenever happiness sneaks into my "little heart." I'm afraid a letter filled with happiness risks never being written, so let me write to you without conditions; don't deprive me of the sense of satisfaction I used to get when addressing you. Today marks eleven years since the day you were gone, but only now am I starting to realize how dearly I miss you, how your loss is too awful a beast to conquer. You know you are sorely needed. My only solace is that I know you feel my thoughts.

Life has become more painfully complex than getting a good grade in history or going out with Aunty Karama's family. Life is never that simple. What to tell you? Gaza is frustrating these days—well, these years. It's a good exercise in patience, at least. This summer is the worst of all the summers that passed without you; breathing some good air has become a luxury we cannot always afford. When nothingness takes over, which happens quite too often, I sit in my room, which is fully exposed to the sun, gazing at the tiny mark of the gunshot and the ugly crack it left there. Yes, that very same crack on the wall caused

by his rifle. Such an eyesore! Other times, I would gaze at it trying to recall how that soldier might look like. That huge creature
grabbed you out of my bed and didn't give you the chance to
finish my bedtime story. I cannot remember anything but his
dusty, black boots and the frightening rifle. So many times, I
tried to imagine how he would look like and always ended up
believing he is no more than a faceless monster. Maybe I have
gone too far, thinking of him, of his life, of his family, of his wife
whom he "loves," of his smart kid who can get a good grade in
math, of him laughing and crying. Baba, what would make this
kind of human rejoice over the fact that I am living the agony of
being fatherless, with an uncompleted story?

It is when darkness prevails that I sit by the window to look
past all those electricity-free houses, smell the sweet scent of a
calm Gazan night, feel the fresh air going straight to my heart,
and think of you, of me, of Palestine, of the crack, of the blank
wall, of you, of Mama, of you, of my history class, of you, of
God, of Palestine—of our incomplete story. I enjoy bringing
to my mind your tender voice narrating the story of Thaer. I
still remember how I cheerfully beamed when you told me that
Thaer and I are so much alike, that he has my wild eyes, and I
his sheepish smile. I have not yet known who he is or where in
life he stands, but I believe I had always trusted your heroes. I
can never forget how your dazzling eyes had brightened when
you recalled him planting some olive seedlings in the backyard
of the orphanage. God bless the smile on your face. God bless
the seeds under the ground. I can never forget how you looked
me in the eyes and said, "He is a boy who lost his whole family
to death but never lost faith in life. I want you to be as strong."
Baba, do you remember when I asked you if he was strong
enough to wrestle an Israeli soldier? You grinned—you always
did—but you didn't answer me. You wanted me to figure things
out on my own. You told me he was only twelve years old when
one of the orphanage girls, Amal, started trembling, hallucinat-
ing, and sweating, but nobody there had the guts to break the
military curfew—to die. Thaer, however, did go out to bring a

doctor for Amal, and then…. And then hell on earth, Baba. And then you are no more.

I don't remember when exactly I started to care about completing Thaer's story, but whenever I ventured to think of giving it a proper ending, I would get tired, and the weight in my head would grow heavier. I could not do it on my own. I thought I had to think twice: once for me, and once for you. I have tried my best, Baba. Doing so was not easy, nonetheless. Of all the people around me, you know best that it takes two to complete a story; it always does. I hated the fact that I might have been driven by curiosity and the sheer love of endings. Thaer is another "you" in my life, just like your photo that stands above the repugnant crack, and your kufiya, whose rich black was worn out to a glorious gray. They are all living parts of you. I had to believe that it is the fear of losing yet more of my father that pushed me there.

I thought, once I thought, of your soul mate, Mama. I thought you must have talked to her about Thaer. I imagined you both had spent nights admiring his eyes and smile, for I can clearly remember when you got together, which was some kind of a luxury for Mama, talks between you did not end. I sometimes travel to specific memories. I hear the timbre of your voice and the echoes of Mama's laughter—laughter which died long ago. But don't you worry; Mama never fails to smile. I know I shouldn't bother you, Baba, but you've got to know that every passing day, Mama is getting frailer. I always wonder, "What does she know which I don't and makes her go on in a life of bitter loneliness?" She must know much, right?

Thinking that she knew Thaer, I once plainly asked her, "What happened to Thaer, in the end?" She washed the last dish, turned the tap off, and stared at the sink for some time. I felt like she was about to give me the healing answer. But she at once retracted. "Who's Thaer?" she asked, narrowing her eyes.

"Thaer," I answered. Then seeing uneasiness drawn on her face, I repeated, "Thaer. My father's Thaer!" In every move she made and every word she didn't say, I could see the glint of a story in the distance. She used her silence to shield the chaos I spotted in her eyes. "Mama! Thaer, the strong kid who planted olive trees at the orphanage." I went on trying to get her to talk. "Strong, huh? It doesn't matter how strong you are or pretend to be, life is going to get to you sometimes and that doesn't make you weak, sweetheart; it makes you human."

I know, Baba, you don't know this new woman; I don't either. I like to call it wisdom. Mom has become cynical, unfortunately, but she gained a lot of wisdom nonetheless. Believing that her answer had nothing to do with your Thaer, I asked her again if she knew what happened to him and whether he got back to the orphanage or not. "He got back home, indeed. We all will," she whispered under her breath. I spent that night thinking of Thaer's home, of the distant life in Mama's eyes. I kept wondering what's more torturous: the awful buzz of the drone outside or the sounds of some tough questions inside. I guess I eventually slept with no answer, thanking the drone for not giving my inner uproar any chance to abate.

Two weeks ago, Grandfather went out with Abu Feras, a neighbour, to get the UNRWA food coupons. He left home sane and returned crazy. That simple. Abu Feras says Grandpa waited three solid hours under the burning sun in the long queue. When he finally was about to get the coupon, he asked the man there, "What are you offering me?" His answer was simple: "Food!"

"And when exactly am I going to get my Jaffa with this coupon?" Grandpa cried out. You can imagine what kind of hullabaloo took place, but everything calmed down when Abu Feras forced him back home. I don't like to think much of the incident. I know that ever since you've been gone, his life is entirely devoted to the grief over a lemon tree and a dear son. Now, he is no longer the man I would talk to for hours. He doesn't believe anymore—doesn't believe in me. He says people fight and die to regain our Palestine. But those freedom fighters don't come back, nor does Palestine. He swears you are now in Jaffa sitting by a lemon tree, enjoying the sun disappearing into the blue of our marvelous sea. Grandfather says you would never come back, for who on earth could leave the paradise of Jaffa? I am, day after day, falling in love with the years that dwell in his wrinkled face and the memories of the old days which are the beats of his weak heart.

You have to expect that I asked Grandfather about Thaer. He immediately replied, "Thaer refused to share a breath with this dirty world. He chose to grow up somewhere else. Don't give me that ridiculous face. Yes, dead people do grow up, but don't you ever believe that they grow older." This answer was even more confusing than Mama's.

"I don't believe you. Thaer could have never considered death as an option. And what about Amal? Was he selfish enough to leave her to die?" I cried.

"Who is Amal?" Grandpa asked with no sense of concern.

For some reason, I felt relieved. I smiled and answered, "My grown-up friend. You should meet her some time." I told him I intended to visit Aunty Karama the next day and asked if he would like to come. He said he could no longer tolerate children and full houses. I couldn't care less. I kissed his forehead. It smelled like the fragrance of lemon blossoms. I felt like he planted a lemon orchard in his cavernous wrinkles. Baba, how could he dare say Thaer was dead? He himself couldn't believe it. I celebrated every new moment added to Thaer's life. I had to be thankful for my faith, for you have to make that leap of faith if you ever want to heal. Years may be the length of one's life, but faith is, undoubtedly, the width.

The next day I woke up really early. I, for my very first time, watched the sunrise. With the dimmed light around me, the world looked just like how I felt. And that was when I looked deep, deep down and started to break apart. Not because I wanted to, but because I couldn't stop. I started to wonder if the things I am living for are worth dying for. I started to think of everything I had in life. Although I have lots of things, they never seemed to be necessary. Every time I think I had it the way I really fancy, it twists and turns and slips away. I didn't feel your soul around. Though I tried to dream you closer, it stayed away just like before. I knew it was about Thaer. I was afraid that I would fall asleep again knowing that he'll always be the story with no ending. I knew that you were just a story away. A story away!

Because I could no longer wait to know what happened to Thaer, I spared the sun two hours to take its favorite place in that awe-inspiring sky. The weather had not yet decided its attitude. The cool air was deceiving, so I put your glorious kufiya around my neck, and I unwaveringly went out. I trusted life that day. Grandfather might think that's naïve, but you wouldn't, I believe. Life is one of the few that is trustworthy.

They say, "To find something, anything, a great truth or a lost pair of glasses, you must first believe there will be some advantage in finding it." And what an advantage, Baba! When I finally reached Aunty Karama's house, I knocked on the door impatiently. I waited more than ten minutes outside. Nobody answered my continuous knocks. I was about to return home when Aunty opened the door. She was asleep. How could she sleep while I didn't know where Thaer's story ends? She welcomed me inside, and excused me to change her clothes. "Please, don't!" I hastily replied to her apology.

She raised her eyebrows, turned pale, and said, "What's the matter with you? Something wrong must have happened to your grandfather, or what on earth could bring you this early when you haven't visited me in months. Oh God! What happened to him?"

I had to calm her down and drive away her worries. "It's Thaer who brought me this early," I said. Yes, Baba. I asked Aunty Karama. I had to, for I knew she was your closest friend ever since you were a little kid who couldn't spell "Palestine." She always prides herself on the fact that she taught you to spell it just right. You had always believed in its bigness. "P for passion, A for aspiration, L for life, E for existence, S for sanity, T for trust, I for You, N for nation, E for exaltation." And then you wrote it just right. You wrote it everywhere you could—on walls, on tables. You carved the stunning letters into trees, and ended up with them engraved in your heart.

"What about Thaer?" she bluntly answered my direct question. Hope found its way back to my heart to congratulate me on the fact that Aunty did know Thaer.

"I mean what happened to him in the end? Did he manage to get his way back to the orphanage? Did Amal survive?" I asked, but she chose not to give an answer. Truth be told, I was disappointed. I felt you didn't trust my heart; you didn't want me to get any closer to your story.

She returned dressed in black and said, "Get up, we are going somewhere special."

With my teary eyes, I gazed at her and said, "Where on this part of the planet is there somewhere special?" She got angry at my answer and said that I am not worthy of knowing Thaer in the first place if I didn't believe in this part of the planet. You have to know that I felt ashamed.

We eventually left. She took me to places I have never been to. The narrow, dark roads of the camp captivated my heart. I felt that bittersweet sensation. I felt you were there. I was sure you were there. On our way to the "special place," Aunty Karama didn't stop talking about every single family in the camp. Stories of deep agony were our companions. I asked her how she could know all these stories; she said that our Nakba is no secret. I admired her more than ever. In my eyes, she had been no more than a dull history teacher. It was the first time I knew that she refused to get promoted, to be more than a third grade teacher. She believed in children. She said she couldn't leave the hope that resides in their pure, little hearts.

"Here we are," she said. I was totally surprised. Was it even a "place"? I went in speechless. Aunty Karama seemed to enjoy the remnants of a burned house. A scent coming out of the earth enveloped me. I couldn't wave it away. Aunty's smiling silence started to press heavier on my heart. I lost sense of place. I'm nowhere. I'm everywhere. I'm here.

Aunty's fruity voice finally came to life such that you wouldn't believe it had ever been silent: "Goodness! Can't you feel it? Your father spent his entire youth teaching the kids here to spell Palestine. P for passion, A for aspiration, L for life, E for existence, S for sanity, T for trust, I for You, N for nation, E for exaltation."

I, for a few seconds, was afraid that she too had gone crazy. "Which kids, Aunty? Your special place is no more than a wasteland," I spoke finally. She swallowed what seemed to be a great deal of anger. She went back to the ruins. She smiled. She laughed. She cried. She went on sighing. "Now what does your place have to do with Thaer and Amal?" I interrupted her on-going sighs.

"You know what, Mariam? You blew it. However, I have always believed life is about second chances. You hardly ever deserve them, but at some point we all need them." She tenderly replied to my rudeness. She went on, asking me, "If you prayed for courage, does God give you courage, or the chance to be courageous? If you prayed for truth, does God give you His truth in your hand, or the chance to open your eyes?"

"Life takes work, I believe," I briefly answered.

"Then open your eyes, sweetheart. Look past the burned house. You'll find the answer by yourself. I believe in you. I believe in whomever your father told the story of Thaer," she said, smiling at my teary eyes. I couldn't see anything, Baba. Nothing caught my bleeding heart. I felt ashamed. I felt you deserved a better successor.

I lowered my head to the ground. I smiled. I laughed. I cried. I kept on sighing at the sight of the olive tree standing alive at the very end of the burned house, of the orphanage. Thaer's seeds grew up. Nothing else was left, but the tree was enough for me, for Amal, for Thaer, and for you, my dearest Baba.

It is when darkness prevails that I sit by the window to look past all those electricity-free houses, smell the sweet scent of a calm Gazan night, feel the fresh air going straight to my heart, and think of you, of me, of Palestine, of the orphanage, of the olive tree, of you, of Amal, of Mama, of you, of my history class, of Aunty Karama, of you, of God, of Palestine, of Thaer's story.

One War Day

by Mohammed Suliman

As usual, Hamza leaned back against the white wall, recently smudged with the hands of his little nephews, nieces, and cousins, and where crevices of various lengths lay bleakly. He fought off all nudging thoughts which overran him every now and then, as if they conspired with the intermittent blasts to preoccupy his mind when it seemed peaceful enough for him to proceed with his reading. These thoughts, he assumed, were of his own creation; they were figments of his own imagination. Therefore they haunted no one but him; they wanted to prevent him from reading his book.

The candlelight flickered, and thus his shadow on the wall did as well, while a gentle, cold breeze blew through the slightly opened windows. Hamza's mother, a woman in her late forties with a mole on her nose, made sure to open them before everyone falls asleep so that, in case a blast takes place nearby, the windows will not be smashed into pieces.

Hamza, his book lying open in his warm hands, persisted in reading his tattered book, which his father used to be obsessed with. As Hamza was reading, he raised his eyes off the book, looked through the open window and said, "They may take our lives, but they'll never take our freedom." He could not tell what exactly brought those words to his mind, but he repeated them a second time, trying to suppress his enthusiasm so that he doesn't wake up his only brother, Jihad, seven years younger than him, who was sleeping nearby. Hardly had Hamza closed his lips on softly pronouncing the "m" in "freedom," than a deafening blast struck the area and turned the once never-ending, prevailing silence into an ear-shattering thunder. Instinctively tightening his grip on the book, his heart pounding as though it were ripping his chest from inside, Hamza immediately jerked his head back. Jihad moved in his sleep, causing his sheets to fall off his bed. Hamza stood up quietly, put the sheets back on his brother, and returned to his book. He focused his gaze ahead, straining to fathom something of what he saw. But the deeper he focused, the more his grip tightened around the book, and the blacker the darkness seemed around him. He soon fell asleep.

No one could ever understand what made him smile in his sleep. No one could ever guess that, only when he was asleep, he could have the things that would grant him relief and happiness. He could own what he was always dispossessed of when not sleeping. He was encircled by his hissing nephews, nieces, and cousins. They were staying at his home along with their families during the war, and now they were competing to see who would come nearest Hamza's sleeping body and touch his bristly beard. Hamza opened his eyes to innocent, joyful faces grinning at him. Yawning, he outstretched his arms, his book next to his head, half-covered under the pillow, and smiled back at the children before he asked them to leave the room. "C'mon, buddies, go play," said Hamza quietly, pulling the blanket up. The sun was streaming into the room through the wide-open windows. This was the first thing his mother did when she woke up. She inherited this habit from her mother, not knowing what exactly it meant to do it in the morning before anything—perhaps to breathe new life into their faces, perhaps the windows were the first objects to meet her eyes, or perhaps to release them from a smell that was not pleasant in the least. The light made the spots on the wall distinctly visible and brightened the heaped-up waxy pieces on the tarnished candlestick.

Seeing that the children were enjoying their game, Jihad signaled to the little ones to come back again. His little angel-like niece stealthily drew near the sleeping Hamza, whose smile had not vanished yet. She moved forward on tiptoe, her eyes beaming, and concealing her smile with the back of her hands, she placed herself by her uncle's head. The little ones started to lose control of their snickers, as they turned into uneasy chuckles. Hamza fidgeted, while the girl, who was blocking the sun from his face, extended her hands to touch his beard. Dreadful silence prevailed in the place and the little ones finally ceased giggling, carefully watching their playmate triumph over her uncle's beard. The little girl fixed her eyes unflinchingly on her target while her hands were steadily nearing Hamza's face. A sudden, huge, piercing blast hit the nearby area. The girl shuddered, pulling her hands promptly. She pushed her bottom lip out and cried. Hamza, who had gotten up panicky, dashed to the windows. He collected himself again and patted his favorite little niece, urging her to stop crying.

Hamza assured himself that he would not have the least trouble, in case, one day, he became a father and his children ask him to tell them a story. He was standing by the window and reflecting on the past few days. "One week! Oh, time goes by so slow," Hamza muttered, resting his head in his hands which were resting on the windowsill. He looked at the vacant street below, recalling how lively it used to be, and feeling queasy, he raised his head. The view of the blue sky dotted with a few light clouds moving overhead amused him; it revived his low spirits. "At least, *you've* got some life," he muttered again, lowering his head. The street was not totally vacant; two stray dogs trotted along, lolling their tongues and wagging their tails. Hamza, delighted, opened his mouth to call the dogs. He wanted to say something, he wanted to call them, and for a moment, he had a sincere desire to yelp. But his desire had not lasted for long. He

raised his head again; the sound of hovering overhead was difficult to ignore. He focused his eyes on the two choppers tearing
their way through the clouds as the two dogs below stood in
the middle of the street. Hamza was mindful enough to discern
the message of both the hovering choppers above and the wagging dogs below. He was reflecting on his unchanging status,
and exasperated at grasping the discrepancy between his own
status, and that of the sky and earth. He had an unequalled ca-
pability to dig deeply into the happenings around him, and little
unimportant incidents which were insignificant to others, profoundly inspired him, though he thoroughly failed to notice his
mother calling out for him to eat his lunch—or else Jihad and
the little ones would eat it up, she joked.

It grew darker, and thus harder to read, as the sun peacefully, sank to bestow a new life on other people. Hamza, sinking
into the darkness, struggled to read the dark lines lying life-
lessly before him. It dawned on him earlier that as long as we
sought life, we could give it, and there always must be life close
to us, closer than we imagine. He had some life to live among
darkness; Hamza had not failed to see it lying before him.
"Everybody has fallen asleep. That's another thing to be proud
of," he thought, relaxing his eyes. Looking down at the page, he
entertained a series of thoughts. The occasional creaks coming
from the farthest door on the other side could not disturb him
from his prolonged musings. "Well, I've got a lot to be proud of,"
he said to himself, conceitedly.

Then, suddenly, "Hey, you're still awake!" came the soft, low
voice of his brother Jihad.

Hamza kept quiet for a moment. "Yeah, just reading a few
pages before I go to sleep," he whispered, smiling at his brother
as he uttered his words.

"Oh, yeah, I know," Jihad whispered back. He moved closer,
his blanket over his shoulder dragging on the floor, and seated
himself next to Hamza. Hamza commenced scanning his book,
his legs lying half-bare as the folds of his slacks piled up at his
knees. Jihad, noting this, drew the blanket to shield his brother's

legs; he could feel they were threatened, though he did not know by what. Covering them would help him or, at the very least, help his brother's concentration.

Even in good, tranquil times, Jihad was afraid of darkness. He hated silence and never liked being cold. He avoided the three conditions when alone, but in the presence of Hamza, he braved the darkness with his laughs. He turned his face, gazed at Hamza, and anxiously observed his eyes were fixed.

Cold air wafted across their faces. Jihad felt a great desire to break the horrifying silence, so, confidently, he interrupted his brother's feigned reading. He stated in a clear, loud tone, "I won't go to school. When the war's over." He grinned.

Hamza, immediately, turned his face and lowered his gaze to meet his brother's. "You won't?"

Widening his eyes in astonishment, he whispered. "Yeah, they say it's going to be an open week," Jihad attempted cunningly. "And I know what they're going to tell us, so I'll just stay home," Jihad continued, his eyes beaming through darkness.

Hamza was not surprised by his little brother's clear and confident statement. "I see; you don't need to go," he said. "But you won't spend that week playing, will you? I'll bring you another two stories. How does that sound?" Hamza went on, admiringly, his smile broadening as he said this.

Jihad exchanged looks with him for moments, and, neglecting the cold darkness, he said cheerfully, "Yeah, I'll read whatever you bring me." He then, feeling secure, sank under his blanket and, soon enough, fell asleep. Encompassed by silent, cold darkness, Hamza thought about the bright future awaiting Jihad. He swore under his breath to make every effort he could to make that happen.

Hamza whiled the night away, his book in his lap, his hands flipping the pages, one after the other. He had not known he would have such persistence during a night spent with no company except that of cold darkness and the amusing wheezing of his little sleeping brother, a persistence that empowered him to satiate his hunger lavishly by devouring the words mercilessly. He breathed a thoroughly new life into himself.

Hamza strove to open his eyes a few hours later. He failed, but, persistent, he had to fight. He failed again, expectedly. His smile never vanished from his lips while sleeping; this time, however, it was the smirk he used to shoot others when they attempted to test his will. Hamza opened his eyes. But all he could see were blurry figures floundering before his eyes—wildly swinging figures, higher and lower, lower and higher, right to left, and left to right. Shortly afterwards, the figures calmed down, and the image settled. Hamza could make out some unfamiliar people around him. He focused his eyes and attempted to take a close look: masked surgeons were encircling him, and on both sides, he could see needles, surgical blades, scalpels, handles, and some scattered tablets. He knew this was a surgery room, but he still needed to ask what kind of room it was and who these people were who stood before him, curious gazes in their eyes. Hamza attempted to ask, but scarcely had his lips separated when huge pains swelled through his chest and the back of his head. He knew he had to submit.

His eyes closed, and he began to remember the last moments he had lived before finding himself in the surgery room. "Right here, c'mon, c'mon! Here, I found another one!" The words resonated in his ears. Hamza, then, amid the clamor, felt himself being heaved from under the rubble, his head hanging limply, and the rubble scratching his dangling hands. The ambulance sirens were disturbing, and he could feel cold air bitterly blow into his face while the hands of those carrying him on each side unconsciously nudged him in the ribs as they rushed to one of the ambulances. Meanwhile, through a gap in the ruins, Hamza saw the little body of Jihad lying serenely, his burned hand extended motionlessly on his tattered book.

Spared

by Rawan Yaghi

THE ELECTRICITY WAS OUT. THERE WAS NO STUDYING TO DO AND we were bored of staying at home. My neighbors and my friends went out for a football match. I wasn't allowed out, because my mother was preparing lunch and it was almost done. I stood on the balcony, watching my friends kicking the ball to each other and acting like famous football players when they scored a goal, spreading their arms like eagles and running around screaming, "Goooooaaaal!"

I stood there, cheering whenever my best friend, Ahmed, scored. Lunch seemed to take forever! I looked back. Mom was putting plates on the table. She looked at me and smiled serenely. She knew how much I wanted to go out and that I was staying because she made me.

"Come on, Mom! Hurry! Ahmed is scoring all the goals," I complained.

"Almost done, dear. You won't be able to play on an empty stomach, will you?" she said sweetly. I gave her a grumpy face and went back to watching the huge match. I rested my chin on the edge of the balcony, pulled my arms back, and kept my feet on the small, blue, plastic stool which my mother bought exactly

51

for that purpose. She said I didn't need more than ten centimeters to be able to view the street. Anything higher than that would cause a tragedy that no one in the family or the neighborhood, especially me, wanted to see. She terrified me with stories about children who climbed the balcony and ended up in the street with all sorts of broken bones. My little mind, of course, believed every single word she said, and I was always cautious not to dangle my head and arms when I climbed the balcony on the precious little stool. Ahmed, who seized a lull in the match, looked up at me and gestured a question. I shook my head and yelled, "Not yet!" The kids laughed at me and went back to their ball.

In a second, a huge light flashed right in front of me, and I was thrown back to the wall of the kitchen and then to its floor. Bricks hit the ground and smashed glass followed seconds later. My knees and hands were shaking, and I couldn't stand up for a moment. There was a strange noise in my ears that sounded like a very annoying, nonstop whistle. Smoke was suffocating me. My mom ran to me, crying hysterically. She checked every part of my body to make sure I wasn't hurt. Then she hugged me. But I did not care; I wanted to see what happened to my friends. She immediately pulled herself up and carried me out of the house, because smoke kept rushing in. My hands were shaking, and my mind couldn't let go of the fact that all of my friends were playing in the street seconds ago. In a minute, my mother and I were standing in the middle of the street, trying to breathe some oxygen, but all we were doing was gulping cement-filled air and coughing it back.

As the smoke faded away, we could finally breathe air that smelled like fireworks. Then my mother realized we were standing in the spot where the game was taking place. She didn't know where to go. She kept walking in circles while holding my head above her shoulder, close to her neck. I saw my friends lying on the ground. All of them. Ahmed was thrown on top of his cousin. His head was torn open. Aunt Um Ahmed saw him as well from the front of her house and started screaming.

My mother was still hugging me as hard as her scratched arms could. Um Ahmed rushed to the street, screaming, carried her son, and hurried for any of the ambulances whose sirens were wailing in the distance. She couldn't get further than a few meters. She collapsed to the ground, still crying, still holding her son, and then she fainted. Ahmed's dad rushed after her. He carried Ahmed and started running. He too couldn't go on. He fell down. By then I was weeping hysterically, along with my mother, who kept carrying me and pulling my head back. She did not want me to get closer to my friends. She wanted to cover my eyes from all of the flesh scattered here and there.

The neighbors carried Ahmed and rushed with his dangling body to an ambulance. They took his mother to one of the neighbors' houses. Uncle Abu Ahmed stood in the middle of the street while people were collecting rubble and evacuating the injured. He stood there, staring at Ahmed's blood and brain on the cement. My father and others tried to pull him away, but he kept resisting them. Later I had to be rushed to the hospital too, as it turned out I was injured.

Ahmed was gone. The others haunted me with their blaming looks every day I went to school. I couldn't look at them. Amputated limbs. Scarred faces. Limping gaits. Our neighborhood was blown to smithereens in a split second. No more games were played. No more goals. No more cheering. And my friends grew up in one second. They no longer looked at me the same way they used to before that awful day. They wouldn't come out to play. And they had a distant look, like Uncle Abu Ahmed when he looked at me, like I didn't understand, like they knew something I did not know, like I did something wrong.

Canary

by Nour Al-Sousi

THE SUN WAS OVERHEAD. THE WEATHER WAS BLISTERING HOT.

He sat on a wooden bench in the middle of a park, like a stranger who got lost at an airport. He counted the lines of his palms as if he noticed them for the first time. He seemed like someone who just woke up and tried to make sense of the surroundings. He scanned the park nervously. He watched a small flight of birds, but soon lost interest as he could not identify their species. He watched a child who, trying to impress his mother, acted like a famous soccer player skillfully dribbling a ball. He smiled. He was in a similar situation before. It felt like déjà vu. He used to beg his mom to take him out with her and even tried to carry heavy things, just to show her he was old enough to lift some of the UN supplies she and his brother Ghassan brought home. She looked behind her and grinned, the smile shrinking the wrinkles of the misery inscribed on her face. In a last desperate attempt, he clutched at the hem of her gown.

"I want to go with you," he insisted, suppressing a sob. "I want to go like Ghassan."

"Mom, he is old enough to carry. He carried two of the three chairs yesterday," argued Ghassan in support of his younger brother.

"Okay, maybe you can go next time. You stay at home today," replied his mother.

Two tears dropped from his eyes as he saw them leave. He then decided to wait outside and tried to convince himself that it was the right thing to do. Someone had to stay home, after all. His mother's promise gave him hope, and Ghassan's support raised his morale. At last, his older brother believed in him.

His mother returned home around noon, carrying a white flour bag with blue stripes. Ghassan would follow proudly, struggling with two plastic bags whose contents would sustain them for weeks to come. He ran to them and gestured to Ghassan to let him carry the two bags. Ghassan, however, offered him only one, the lighter of the two; he did not want his brother to fail his first test carrying the bags. He carried the bag with his left hand, then with his right one, then with the left hand again. When his hands got tired, he hugged it hard. He did not want to let go; he did not want to let his brother down.

◊

She stood gazing at him from afar, examining his facial expressions and gestures that, to her disappointment, looked strange yet familiar; she could not locate them inside her mind. Her eyes unblinkingly fixed on him. She roamed the park, forming a circle with him at the center. She thought it would help her dig deep into her mind if she examined him from three dimensions. She failed. As she stood in front of him, a kid jumped in front of her, playing in front of his proud mother, showing off his soccer skills. She shook her head. She was in a similar situation, so similar that it felt like déjà vu. She was a little kid in her cold house trying to please her mother and begging her to stay. She felt so lonely and so cold. Her only solace was the many dolls and teddy bears she had in her bedroom. They were her world, and her hope. Her mother would leave the house to return back around dawn, carried by a new boyfriend.

◊

The sun was overhead. The weather was stifling.

He laid his head back against the bench, checked his watch, and closed his eyes to relieve them from the sweltering heat. He collected his saliva and swallowed it in an attempt to fight a sudden surge of thirst. Then, when he decided to think of something refreshing, her golden hair caught his attention. She was short and the army uniform made her look even shorter. She was gorgeous—that he could not deny. He watched her circling the park. He thought to himself, "Maybe she is from Bologna. Would I be able to like her if she were a tourist?" Then he lost interest. The noise of the traffic and people around him invaded his thoughts, bringing a memory of a similar noise. He was running with his brother to the UNRWA water truck to bring fresh water. The camp did not have fresh water for days. They queued for an hour or so, filled up two jerry cans, lifted them on their shoulders, and staggered on their way back home at the edge of the camp. Attracted by the sound of a bird, he put down the jerry can and wanted to chase it, a hobby they pursued whenever their mother was away from home.

"It's a canary!" yelled Ghassan. "I saw it first," he said. "I can get it for you if you wait here," Ghassan said. The canary flew into the bushes of the outskirts of the nearby Jewish settlement. It took only one gunshot. His brother and the canary were silenced forever, in front of his eyes.

◊

She observed how he, eyes still closed, relaxed on the bench apparently unconcerned by anyone. She wondered what he was thinking of amidst this noise. She wondered if he was on a date. Struck by the glare of the sun, she decided to circle the park around him once more. She looked at him one more time when she was stuck by a piercing flash of a Star of David dangling from a chain around his neck. She looked away and closed her eyes very hard to get rid of the momentary blindness that took her by surprise. She felt her brain had evaporated by the heat, driving her insane. She wished he had been waiting for her. And just when she felt desperate, something inside her made her love this state of hallucination. She sped towards a nearby tree to spare herself the flaming air around her. She decided to think of something refreshing. She closed her eyes and imagined him relaxing in a tub of cold water, with it dripping from his hair, nose, and ears. His face was distracting her. He had on his face things she had been looking for. What they were, she did not know. She felt she had to reach out to him, to occupy his world. She remembered when she last had a boyfriend. That was long ago, she thought. That was a little before she was recruited in the army. It was not easy for both of them to stay together having to serve in totally different places. He could have tried harder, she thought.

◊

The sun was overhead, the air bearing down.

Sweat tiptoed down his forehead to his temples. He lifted his left hand to wipe it away. He opened his eyes and looked around. To his relief, the mother and her son were finally gone and more soldiers were gathering for the lunch break at the usual place. So far, everything was going as planned. The belt was stifling him, and his hands were damp. The sweat was pouring from him, but he needed to focus and see clearly. He dried his hands, wiped the sweat off his forehead, checked the timer in his right pocket, readjusted his heavy jacket and drew it closer to his body as if winter came abruptly. He checked the time again; it was almost 1:10 p.m.

She opened her eyes and seeing him about to stand, decided to act on impulse and go talk to him. It was her last chance. She lost many people because she was not daring enough; not this time, she thought. She walked toward him.

As he raised his head to examine the area one last time, his worst fears materialized in front of him. The short blonde in khakis and black army boots, gun strapped on her back, ponytail dancing behind her, was darting through the tables towards him. He stood, sweating even more, paralyzed with surprise. He could barely move his hand into his pocket to clutch at the trigger.

She was sweltering. He made a move. She quickened her pace. She was finally in front of him, almost two meters away. She stopped to wipe her forehead with the back of her left hand. A drop of sweat rolled down his left cheek to his neck. He shuddered. A drop of sweat went down her forehead. She blinked. The sun was overhead. It was scorching. The Star of David around his neck, his wintery jacket, his Arab looks! She felt dizzy. It all made sense now! How could she not figure that out? She pulled her M16 and clenching tightly on it planted its barrel into his forehead. She sent out a warning call over her walkie-talkie to alarm the rest of the Israeli soldiers and stood motionless, sweat pouring off her.

Their eyes met. Fear and frustration flowed. It filled the place. Her finger was on the trigger. His finger was on the trigger. Death carried them both to the unknown.

The Story of the Land

by Sarah Ali

To Dad

I LOOKED AT HIS TEARY EYES, AND BEHOLDING SOMETHING AKIN to happiness, I smiled. The man I have always known to be my father was back. He did not look like that unfamiliar man whom I could not fully recognize during the last three years. He was no longer that absent-minded, silent figure gazing at walls all the time and uninterestingly nodding whenever addressed by anyone at home. He was there. He was present. He was actually listening as I went on bragging about a high grade of mine. A phone call and a piece of paper signed by some Turkish-sponsored institution brought back my father. I looked at his eyes again, this time more carefully for fear that my first glance was false. As I saw that absolute happiness in my father's eyes, a big smile made it to my face again.

As we now commemorate the Land Day, we honor the people who stood up for their Land in 1976, when Israel announced thousands of Palestinian dunums would be confiscated. During marches held to protest that declaration, six people were killed. The 30th of March brings back a memory of our Land, my father's Land. A couple weeks ago, we got a phone call informing us that my father's name had been selected for a reconstruction program funded by Turkey. The program aims at helping Gazan farmers whose Lands were damaged during the Israeli offensive in 2008 to replant their trees. It provides farmers with all types of facilitating materials, such as fences, tree cuttings, seedlings, seeds, and irrigation systems. My father declined to apply for those organizations that gave financial compensations to farmers. How can he take money in return for Land? Unlike any other aid program, this program gives no money to farmers. It instead helps them stand on their own.

Though my father was born to a family of farmers, he did not follow that path. He studied economics and political science in Egypt and spent most of his youth working as a journalist, mainly a columnist, writing about economic and political issues in newspapers in Kuwait. When he was back in Gaza, though, he had to take care of the piece of Land my grandfather left for him years before. It was not difficult for him. Gradually, the Land became more of a passion than a profession. It was one of the few things he cared about, the daily thing that kept him busy. It was heaven on earth.

During those twenty-three days of the Israeli attack on Gaza, we were constantly receiving news of Land being run over by Israeli bulldozers. We were told thousands of trees were gone. We were told my uncles' trees were gone. We were told our trees were gone. We were told Sharga, the whole district of eastern farmland, was gone. But these were rumors—or so my father wanted to believe. We all had hope that our Land was still intact, totally untouched. We were clinging to the assumption that only *other* people's trees could get uprooted, but certainly not our beautiful, unmatched olives. Certainly not the trees that were, to my father, the only thing he boasted of to prove he was no less of a Gazan than those who repeatedly reproached him for, as they put it, "recklessly leaving the land of black gold" where they assumed he swam in Kuwaiti oil pools every day, and for "coming to live here" with a small "h." My father looked at it quite differently, for Here, he always believed, is the Land of *al-zait al-muqaddas*—the holy oil.

Gaza's sky was blue again. Things were over—the news said things were over. My father went there. He went to check up on the Land. He put his faith in his olives being an exception, and he went there. He put his faith in that little white spot in the heart of the bulldozer's operator who, my father supposed, could not have resisted the beauty of our Land and who listened to his innate, good being that told him not to run over this Land. He had faith in the goodness of Man and he went there. He put his faith in God and he went there. My brother, who accompanied him, told us later that all they saw as they walked was ruined Lands filled with bulldozed, dead trees which seemed to suffice for the families' need of firewood for years to come. My brother said Dad started crying as he saw people crying. They went on. They saw more toppled trees, feeble and defeated. They went on. There was the heaven. The scene of our Land was not shocking. Simply put, our trees were no exception. Our trees were gone. A miscellany of affliction and denial took over the place. My father's faith, I could tell, was smashed into little pieces. The world seemed like an ugly place.

One of our trees, which later became the subject matter the whole neighborhood spoke of, was still standing there. Just one week before the attacks, my father told my brother how slanted this tree was and how quickly they needed to get rid of it. They were planning to cut it, and yet, ironically, it was the only tree the Israeli army left (out of boredom or out of mercy, I cannot tell). But it was still there. Later, whenever my cousins wanted to make Dad feel less terrible about it, they made fun of the whole thing. "How the hell did the soldiers know you were planning to cut it anyway and so decided not to cut it themselves?" my cousins would remark. Everyone would start laughing. But Dad did not. His Land and olive groves are not laughing matters to him.

When my father and brother were home that day, my brother started telling us about what he saw. He told us that the trees were uprooted—"*Al-shajar tjarraf*," he kept repeating. My father was in his room, crying. During the weeks that followed my father's visit to the Land, he had a daily schedule: in the morning, he prayed and read Qur'an. At night, he cried.

Speaking about the Land, the houses, and generally the financial losses during or right after the Israeli offensive would have sounded very selfish and indifferent to others. When people are dying, you do not speak of your beautiful house that was leveled to the ground. When people are losing their legs and arms, leaving them disabled for the rest of their lives, you do not speak of your fancy car that once looked like a vase adorning the streets of your modest neighborhood and that is now a gray wreck. When a mother is burying her child before she could say good-bye, you do not speak of your Land and your trees that were mercilessly uprooted. Those people speak. They cry. They mourn. You listen. And for the memory of your insignificant, little misery, you grieve in silence. And that seemed to have amassed more agony over Dad's pain.

Recently, I went to father to get accurate information about the trees that were uprooted, their numbers, and their age.

"Why are you asking? Are you applying for one of those charity institutions that offer some money and a bag of flour instead of helping people plant their trees again? Are you? We do not need those! The guy I met from the reconstruction program called last week, and they already sent laborers and farmers to start their job. Do you still want to apply for charity?"

"No, Baba! I am just writing something for my blog."

"Blog? Okay, whatever that is!"

"So, how many trees were uprooted? 180 olive trees I guess and...?"

"189 olive trees. 160 lemon trees. 14 guava trees..." he bellowed, angry that I missed the exact number.

Embarrassed, I lowered my head and wondered why I was doing this to myself. My thoughts were interrupted when he went on, "Next time you decide to do whatever it is that you want to do right now, get your numbers straight!"

I made no reply.

"You hear me? They were 189 olive trees. Not 180. Not 181. Not even 188. 189 olive trees."

He left the room a few minutes afterwards. Guilt was all I could feel.

That an Israeli soldier could bulldoze 189 olive trees on the Land he claims is part of the "God-given Land" is something I will never comprehend. Did he not consider the possibility that God might get angry? Did he not realize that it was a tree he was running over? If a Palestinian bulldozer were ever invented (Haha, I know!) and I were given the chance to be in an orchard, in Haifa for instance, I would never uproot a tree an Israeli planted. No Palestinian would. To Palestinians, the tree is sacred, and so is the Land bearing it. And as I talk about Gaza, I remember that Gaza is but a little part of Palestine. I remember that Palestine is bigger than Gaza. Palestine is the West Bank; Palestine is Ramallah; Palestine is Nablus; Palestine is Jenin; Palestine is Tulkarm; Palestine is Bethlehem; Palestine, most importantly, is Yafa and Haifa and Akka and all those cities that Israel wants us to forget about.

Today I came to realize that it was not the phone call that brought my father back, nor was it the paper signed by the aid institution. It was the memory of the Land being revived that brought him back. It was the memory of olive trees giving that sense of security each time he sat under them, enjoying their shade and dodging the burning rays of the sun. It was the memory of the golden oil, the best and purest oil, being poured into jerry-cans and handed to family and friends as precious gifts. It was the memory of long years of cherishing the Land, years of giving and belonging.

Between my father and his Land is an unbreakable bond. Between Palestinians and their Land is an unbreakable bond. By uprooting plants and cutting trees continually, Israel tries to break that bond and impose its own rules of despair on Palestinians. By replanting their trees over and over again, Palestinians are rejecting Israel's rules. "My Land, my rules," says Dad.

Toothache in Gaza

by Samiha Olwan

I WOKE UP WITH THE SAME AWFUL TOOTHACHE, THE PAIN DRILL-
ing through the top of my head. For two days, I could not study,
I could not eat, and, worse, I could not sleep. Every part of my
body ached in its own way. There was no other choice, then. I
had to go to the dentist. I tried to avoid it, but it was too late.
My father was supposed to make me a dentist appointment.
Unfortunately, I had to wait three more days for an appointment. There's nothing more irritating in the world than having
the headache brought on bay a toothache. It is just unbearable.

Hearing my moaning and my cries of pain, my father yelled
from the other room, "If you can't handle the pain for three
more days, then we can just go to the...."

I think I either did not hear what he said clearly, or I simply
thought he was kidding. I inquired, "To go where?"

Clearing his throat, my father yelled that fearful word
which came out of his mouth sharp and distinctive: *al-wekala*–
the UNRWA Health Center. My heart sank, my whole body
shivered, and my words were stuck in my throat. The image
of the place was suddenly all I saw. Every day on my way to

university, I pass by two buildings of UNRWA, a health center and the headquarters.

The walls of the clinic were whitish with a few blue stripes. They had drawings of very disproportionately painted people being carried away into ambulances. It was not the white and pale blue buildings with the flag of UNRWA or its crude paintings, nor was it the inaccessible barb-wired walls which bothered me whenever my eyes would set on the place. It was rather the scene of the crowds lining up or trying to stay lined up to reach the fenced windows and the voice of the invisible person on the microphone calling for either names or numbers. I always couldn't help but feel sorry for those who had to wait there in queues under the burning summer sun or the heavy winter rain. I never imagined myself lining up for any reason before. Never had I thought I would be standing there waiting for my name to be called and struggling to get to the fenced window with the hope that I would be one of those lucky enough to be called.

Though I wanted to wait out the trauma I was passing through, the unprecedented pain defeated me. I surrendered. The journey to the clinic had to be made whether I liked it or not. After all, how bad would it be to stand there in the lines amongst other people, other average Palestinians, refugees, and patients? It is only a medical center, I tried to console myself, unsuccessfully.

A sleepless night passed. When I went to my father the next day, I didn't have to say a word. He tried to alleviate my panic with a gentle look. He said he had to go to the clinic an hour before me so that he could get me a place before it got jam-packed. How could a place get crowded at seven in the morning, I wondered?

At exactly 8 a.m., I went to the clinic as my father had instructed me. The way to the center brought me much agony. I thought of how inconsiderate I could sometimes be towards my father, how I never fully appreciated what he does for us. He had to stand in line to get us the UNRWA supplies once a month.

We are among the lucky Palestinians who enjoy the advantages of the UNRWA Card, with a capital "C." My mother is a refugee. I never knew why some people looked at that card as a kind of privilege, and I always wondered why some of them hold it with such pride.

The refugee card was and continues to be an insult to remind us of the little that refugees get in comparison with what they have really lost. Would a bag of flour compensate for the farmland they once had? Would a bag of sugar make up for the bitter misery those people have always felt after losing their sweet homes to dwell in refugee camps? Would the two bottles of oil make them forget their olive trees, which had been mercilessly uprooted as they themselves were? Or maybe it is simply a declaration that they are temporary refugees who once had the land which, as long as this card is still in their hands, would still be waiting for them to return. Only a shot of sharp pain brought me back to the present.

When I arrived at the center around 8:30, a few people were lining up outside. I guessed those presumptions and fears were a result of my unexplainable phobia of dentists; I thought I had been exaggerating them. The white and blue building seemed quite a nice place after all. My favorite colors gave me some sort of relief, which unfortunately did not last for long. The voices of people babbling got clearer the moment I entered the clinic. Looking around, I took in the laughably small clinic, which technically was several small rooms with a panel above each door illustrating different kinds of treatment provided by the health center: The General Clinic. The Optometrist. The Dentist. Internal Medicine, which occupied the major part of the clinic.

Thank God, it is only a toothache, I thought.

My father found his way to me among the crowd. "Why are you so late? I got you a number. You were about to lose it," he called from where he was standing.

"No way, not the number. I can't lose the number after all I have been through," I thought, pain preventing me from talking. It was one of those times when one is rendered a number, when one is no longer a human being but a number. I was no longer me. I was Seven. And "Seven" was the only thing I wanted to hear at that moment. Although, seeing all those sick people mildly relieved my tooth pain that started gnawing at my brain and my limbs. I wanted it to stop, by any means.

I sat down on the bench my father reserved for me. Seeing the state I was in, he preferred to stand up like most of the people waiting for their numbers. The five benches available in the room would by no means suffice the tens of women, children, men, and elderly crowdedly standing there. I got a glance at the woman beside me. My eyes caught a glimpse of the number on the card she was gripping with both hands. I was shocked. For how long does she have to wait for number thirty-six when I was number seven and not called yet? Not for long, I discovered later.

"Number six! Number six?" called a bored voice over the loudspeaker.

"Number six? Where's number six?" roared almost every person present, their voices reverberating through the hall. The door of the room opened, and a very old woman crawled out, limping slowly to the right then to the left, two young relatives, apparently her grandsons, holding both her hands. The woman's eyes were closed and cotton was sticking out of her tiny mouth. She clearly was in a lot of awful pain, which, in ways I could not explain, made my own whole body throb. I wanted to peer into the room when a little girl, around ten years old, pushed herself through the crowd into the room and closed the door behind her.

The girl, whose hair was dangling in a long plait, was wearing the white uniform with blue stripes I always hated as a student. (I always wondered whether it was blue with white stripes.) She went into the dentist's room alone. I felt ashamed of myself. She was the younger version of me, except that I had liked to wear my hair in two plaits. And most importantly, she was not as cowardly as to bring her father with her. She was holding her school bag when she got in. So, most probably, she was heading to school after having her tooth removed. In two minutes, the door opened again. The little girl came out with the same look of defiance on her face as if declaring, "I finally got you out of my mouth, you stupid little tooth." I thought of the amount time this little girl spent in there. Two minutes—not even enough to give her any sort of anesthesia....

For a moment, I thought about running away. My father began pushing me through the crowd even before number seven was called. The people present again roared in unison, "Number seven! Where is number seven?" He held my hands while I lagged behind. The three doctors seemed very nice— well, at least they asked me about my name. I had to lie on the chair, and in less than a minute, the doctor declared I needed surgical tooth removal, which, unsurprisingly, the UNRWA clinic did not offer. I forgot about the pain. All I wanted was to get out of that sterile room.

I stopped holding my breath when I was out. I hurried for the exit of the building. When my dad emerged later on, I, with the same smile of the little girl, looked into his eyes, "See, they cannot help me. I told you." My father, who had stayed behind for more information from the doctors and to bring any medications they prescribed, laughed when he saw my pale face finally returned to its usual color. He raised the little bag of medicine in front of my face, "At least, I've got you some painkillers."

"Yes, painkillers!" I smiled thoughtfully.

Will I Ever Get Out?

by Nour Al-Sousi

AND NOW HERE I AM. THE BATTERY INDICATOR ON MY CELL phone is half empty. Hopeless is my case, for the network will not respond to my persistent attempts to call anyone.

This very cell phone was my gift for passing secondary school with distinction; it was my father's way of expressing his overwhelming joy on that day. I remember when he reminded me of my future dream: "Oh, at last! I'll see you as the doctor I always dreamed you'd be, Said. At last, I will!"

I was, then, expected to pursue my university studies abroad, but it seemed that fate wanted it another way. The mere idea of me leaving this country and never coming back again was out of the question for my parents. They wanted me to stay. And I, therefore, had no choice but to join the Faculty of Medicine here, in Gaza. To tell the truth, it was not as bad as I had expected. Not at all. All that had complicated our lives and made them intolerable was nothing other than those regular power failures, the food price crisis, the continuing closure of the borders that kept us from traveling abroad, the transportation crisis, and the desperate struggle for a living. Only these and nothing more.

Oh, how happy those days seem to be when compared to these! Never mind, it won't take longer than an hour more.

A year passed. Our home was shelled. The house was partly damaged. Only one room was totally destroyed. And my father happened to be inside that room.

A year passed, and I still keep myself away from that room. I still smell the burned flesh.

Even here—in my confinement—I smell it.

My agony was so great that it could not be relieved by tears. I didn't cry over the death of my father.

All of a sudden, I had become the family's sole provider. I had to look for work, any work. That, unexpectedly, did not take long as someone hissed in my ears, "Come and work with me, Said. You'll never find a better job than digging the tunnels!"

"But...."

"No buts. It pays double what you will earn anywhere. It is guaranteed all year long," said the man. "And we will call you 'Doctor,'" he added and grinned.

Failing to strike a balance between my study and my new work, I dropped medical school.

The low-battery indicator never stops irking me.

Raising her blessed hands, my mother prayed for me. She prayed for me, not knowing what sort of work I was doing. After all, she couldn't tolerate the idea of her children going to bed with empty stomachs. I could not either.

I took a taxi to Rafah. The digging was taking place under the houses near the border. The only thing I was thinking of was how my body would endure being in a grave more than twenty meters deep. The fifty shekels at the end of the day, and the bags I brought back home that drew smiles on the faces of my mother and little brothers and only sister, made the task a bit easier.

We began digging. It got very stuffy inside. We were three teams: the first team digs, the second team takes the sand out, and the third team holds the scaffolding poles. Although I was masked, the sand could feel its way through the mask into my mouth, and drinking some water worsened the situation. I coughed and coughed. My unmasked mates laughed deeply. "You'll get used to this soon, Doc," someone told me.

I took my mind off them. I envisioned the sea where I used to spend most of my time diving; this was one of my hobbies. One cold drop of sweat awakened me, tearing its way down on my back. Even this little drop was contaminated with sand.

Once I wanted to warn against digging this close to the sea. But I refrained. Those non–medical school tunnel-diggers must know better. The task sounded easy, albeit sweaty, until the sand began falling from the sky—from the dark sky of the dark tunnel. I stayed behind at the end of the tunnel to hold the poles.

I am just wondering how long I have been stuck here in this tunnel. My mates have gone out and left me alone. My mother's prayers have done me no good. The tunnel collapsed over the gate before I could make it out.

They will come to save me from here, for sure.

My cell phone is moaning, its light flickering.

I feel the bitter cold piercing my bones. A spasm of pain. And I feel the warmth of the earth from under my feet as though it were patting me to sleep. In the horizon, there seems to be a light coming from afar. It seems tangible.

A hymn. I can hear a hymn now. My mother's prayer. My sister's empty stomach. The smell of burned flesh. And the flavor of sea water.

A Wall

by Rawan Yaghi

IT'S FUNNY THERE'S A SIDEWALK HERE. I WALKED WITH MY fingertips touching the huge blocks of the great Wall built to scare me. I didn't look at the graffiti; I know it very well. The sky was half eaten by the Wall, and the sun was no better. I tripped on a stone, probably thrown by some of my friends yesterday. I sat down where I stumbled and grabbed the stone, stared at it for a minute, and threw it over the Wall. I listened for an "ouch," a curse word, footsteps, a call, a whisper, or a gunshot. Nothing. I kept on walking. It didn't seem to end. My fingertips were now stained with all the graffiti colors. I stopped. I turned my face to the Wall. I put both my hands on it. I pushed. I kept pushing, my arms straight, my teeth clenched, my legs rooted to the ground, the smell of the spray paint going through my nostrils to my lungs. A man walking past me stopped to see what would come of this. My feet started backing the other way. A sound from inside me broke out into a scream. I collapsed to the ground crying. The man laughed and went on walking.

A Wish for Insomnia

by Nour El Borno

THE STORM HAS BEEN HOWLING THE WHOLE NIGHT, THE WIND whistling through the tiny gaps of the windows and underneath the doors. The clock blinks 2 a.m. The screaming starts. Everyone's up—husband, wife, and their two children. Ezra's thunder-like screams had awakened them. He was sweating profusely. The sweat, coupled with the breeze sneaking through the half-open bedroom door, joined forces, and he felt a cold shiver run through his veins and a sharp pain in his chest.

Ezra, who slept on the left side of the bed for a change that night, stood up, groped his way to the half-shattered mirror, looked at his hands furtively, and then sat on the carpet near the dressing table. He crossed his legs and placed his hands on his knees as if he were carrying something, fixing his gaze unblinkingly on them. His wife, Talia, followed with her eyes every move he made until he sat motionless. She knew what to do next. Before she went to comfort him, she noticed their two children standing in the dimly lit corridor behind the door, their shadows extending like ghosts.

"Go back to your room, sweeties," she whispered to the little ones while leaving her bed. Sarah and Ziva grew accustomed to waking up to their father's shrieks in the middle of the night. They returned to their bedroom, not sure about what had just happened to their father, whose screams were louder this time—louder and more painful. The past few weeks were agonizing for them. Their father did not leave the bedroom. All they saw and heard of him was his screaming in the middle of the night, the noise of things breaking, and his moaning during the day. Their mother always kept them away from him. Talia moved slowly, careful not to startle him. He was trembling, his face pale, his heartbeat racing.

"Another nightmare?" she said gently as she sat opposite him.

"This time was much worse," muttered Ezra, panting.

"What did you see?" she asked again, trying not to sound interrogative, a technique she learned by attending several sessions with their psychiatrist. Dr. David told her that if done properly, making her husband talk about the nightmare could be releasing.

He continued out of habit, rather than consciously responding to his wife's questions. "We were sent in tanks to Gaza, again.... We were instructed to shoot to kill. That was the order. And...and we shot almost every moving thing: we shot the water tanks, a couple of stray dogs, a cow, a dozen people...and there was that woman...with her kid.... I could not tell if she was fat or pregnant. I could not through the night-vision binoculars. I do not know what happened to the kid. I wish I could know now. The kid cried the whole night. I kept hearing the commander's order in the background, but it was the little kid's voice that haunted me everywhere...."

Sensing that her husband was drifting between dream and reality, Talia squeezed his hands in an attempt to bring him back to consciousness.

"Honey, you were doing your duty to your country. It was your job to follow orders. It's alright," reminded the wife, trying to soothe him. He could not hear her. He could not see her. He could not feel her hands touching his.

"The smell of the gunshots, the deep mooing of the cow, and the barking of the dog, the blood on my hands, the whimpers of the woman, and then the cries of the child. The cries of the child. The cries of the child," he kept repeating. He went on, "Some of the guys were taking pictures and some were writing on the walls. Ben and Levi were dancing around, taking souvenirs from each house we broke into. A lot of people from the dream were real. People I already killed." Then there was a momentary silence. He was suffocating. His chest was burning, and his heart almost ripped through it.

Deliberately and gently, Talia ran her fingers through his blond hair and tried to see through his blue eyes. She could see pain. And she could see horror. Obviously, talking was not helping. She thought of abandoning Dr. David's advice.

"We walked into this house," he carried on. "It was dark. Really dark. They said the house has terrorists. He said the house has terrorists. The general said the house had terrorists. I heard him loud and clear."

"Darling, I am sure it's nothing. Just relax...."

"I walked in. I couldn't see. Flashlights. There was no electricity. It was dark. We shot everyone. The electricity went back on. And...when the lights were back on...when the lights were on, the general was dead. Ben and Levi. All dead. Everyone was dead. The guys were dead. A little girl...bleeding. Ziva's bunny. Blood. Our little Ziva...she was...she was dead. I held her in my arms. But she was dead. I killed her with my gun...."

"Daddy, I don't do anything wrong. Why did you kill me?" little Ziva asked, dropping her bunny on the floor.

Bundles

by Mohammed Suliman

AT DAYBREAK, SALMA, A PLUMP, BRUNETTE WOMAN IN HER early forties, was wrapping some bundles of Naji's favorite food and cigarettes. When she finished packing everything into a bundle, she dressed up and prepared herself as well. Confusing feelings occupied her. She didn't know whether she should be in high spirits, as she was, or dejected, as she intermittently felt. It was only a few hours that separated her from seeing her son for the first time in the three years since he was caught in a failed attempt to sneak beyond the borders. During these three years, Salma used to sit where her son kissed her good-bye, weeping and sniffing each of the letters her son sent her. She lived sobbingly reproaching herself for letting him go—as though she had any way to put a stop to what he was up to. She grew more pallid each day as she languished after her lost son. She wept so bitterly over him that her eyes seemed to have been drained of tears. It struck five in the morning, and Salma carried the two bundles and left the house. Her son, who hadn't been on trial yet, was in the Nafha desert prison inside Israel.

Tightly clenching a package in each hand, Salma alighted from the car with anxious thoughts whirling through her head.

She felt ready to drop, but she had to pass one last checkpoint before she could gain access into Israel. After having her neatly organized packages inspected and then messed up, she had to stuff them hurriedly and go through the metal detector. When she passed through it, it gave a buzzing sound. Her blood ran cold. A blond, capped officer with freckles on his face asked her to check if she had any metal pieces or coins with her. Salma examined herself thoroughly but failed to find a sign of any metal. The officer, then, required her to go through the metal detector for a second time. As she returned, Salma felt her heart pounding so loudly, she was sure the smirking officer could hear it. She stepped toward the metal detector and attempted to steady her legs while she passed through it. And then "Zzzzz"—it buzzed again. Immediately, two slender female officers came ambling toward her, when it flashed through her mind: it was the buckle of her watch that made all the fuss. "Good riddance," she said to herself, feeling stupid and happy that she could eventually pass through without the machine buzzing. Salma, cursing the occupation for making her look stupid and awkward, saw the image of her Naji draw nearer and nearer.

◊

It had been three and a half years since Abu Naji passed away of prostate cancer. His wife, Salma, had to contend with the daily life of a depressed family, along with her son, Naji. Naji prematurely became the head, and the only breadwinner, of the family.

Naji was tall and skinny, a young man in his early twenties. He struggled to bring his mother and himself their daily sustenance early in his life. He would get up early every day, pick up the sandwiches his mother wrapped for him, and he would get back late in the evening with a little cash. The new work Naji had obtained at the smuggling tunnels was good enough to bring them food; it was enough to keep them alive for a day or two more, yet it was likely to bring them death.

Salma felt disconcerted while Naji was having his usual modest supper with her at home. Salma took notice of Naji's absent-mindedness. Still staring at his sullen face, she refilled his cup of tea. Naji's eyes were leering at the pastry in his hands, his lower jaw moving up and down as sluggishly as his body appeared to be.

Breaking the silence, Salma asked, "How was your day at work?" fully aware of the answer. "Tiring, I suppose?" she continued. Naji, however, sounded uninterested in his mother's question. He was transfixing his eyes unblinkingly at the small, scattered pieces of sage floating on the surface of the hot tea. It had been a while before Naji realized that his mother was uneasily exchanging with him nervous looks from the edge of her watery eyes. "What's wrong?" she asked him once more.

"Nothing," Naji lied.

"Don't lie to me," she snapped at him. "You've been acting strangely since you came home. What happened? Just let me know," she tersely continued. Naji finally told her what happened between him and his boss, Abu Sham, inside the rotten chamber near the tunnel where he worked.

"It's dangerous. I know," said Naji.

His mother kept silent.

"I'll make 4,000 shekels for a two-day job. I can use the money to start a small enterprise. I can be free," he added convincingly, "I sneak in, bring the package, and then come back."

"Do you even know what that package is?" his mother finally asked.

"I honestly don't know," he replied.

Naji was up early in the morning. Salma was preparing his breakfast when he came in, already dressed. She started singing in a low voice. Her singing was mixed with sporadic heartbreaking sobs. While having their breakfast, Naji cleared his throat and raised his eyes to meet his mother's. "I don't want you to be angry with me. I'm doing this for us," said Naji in a distressed voice. Salma, who was not eating, shot him an angry yet compassionate look. Lowering her face, she said nothing. Naji got up to his feet and headed to where his mother was sitting. "I'll be back in two days; I promise." His mother raised her face again while Naji was grabbing her hands. Salma felt that it was a moment of farewell. It was a moment of inevitability. Naji lowered himself and kissed the back of her hands. Failing to gulp back her tears, Salma tightened her grip of his hands before she let go of them—of him.

◊

Salma finally reached the prison. She entered a big hall; she had never seen anything like it before. Shortly after, she realized she would be inspected again. There was bustling. She heard many loud voices coming from here and there. It seemed like dozens of quarrels were taking place at the same moment. The view of her son was fading in her mind when she found herself in a row of elderly women waiting to hand in their papers.

After what seemed a long while, Salma found herself face to face with a blond female clerk. She was slim and short, and seemed to be sinking in the chair. Salma stood still while the blond clerk sat at a large, glossy desk and spoke as hastily as she typed. She looked up at Salma, and moved all four fingers back and forth next to her thumb at the end of her stretched hand to tell her to hand in the papers. Salma handed her the papers and examined her fingers while they were hitting the keys gently. The officer pushed her papers back to her, and Salma moved hastily to release herself from the restless, nudging women behind her.

Salma didn't have the slightest idea where she should go. She was roaming the place with the bundles in her hands and the papers curled under her arm. She had a passing thought of inquiring about where to go from an officer at one of the gates, but she spotted the nudging woman limping with three huge bags outside the hall. Salma hurried to catch up with her.

"Hello, ma'am," Salma said, doing her utmost to keep up her strides.

"Hello," came the throaty voice of the old woman.

Salma was about to ask where they were supposed to go before the nervous woman's voice came again. "So, visiting your son?"

"Yes," Salma answered, straining to walk by her side. "And you?" she went on.

"Grandsons. Two," the old woman answered her promptly.

"Seeing them now, are we?" asked Salma.

But the old woman broke off to rest from the heavy weight of the three bags before moving on. Salma was waiting for her answer while she was taking short breaths. Then, the old woman said, "Not yet, still have to pass the last inspection." Salma felt disappointed at hearing the word "inspection." She couldn't take the waiting and felt more waves of longing breaking through her body as she made more strides, now behind the old woman. "I know it feels embarrassing, but that's it; we have no chance of seeing our sons if we think about being embarrassed," came the restless voice of the woman again.

Salma thought for a moment the old woman was not talking to her. Then, when she assured herself that she was, she tried to interpret what she meant by "embarrassing" before she replied, "Uh, sorry, but I don't understand what you mean."

The old woman said, "The inspection; I am talking about the inspection."

Salma felt as though she should have felt embarrassed at each of the inspections she went through so far. "What's wrong with them?" she asked, feeling truly embarrassed.

"What? Don't you know?" the old woman looked dumbstruck.

"Know what?" Salma replied, sounding stupefied; her heart was beating fast. The old woman looked at her pityingly. She told Salma that at the last inspection before she could see her son, she had to submit herself to a cavity search in case she was hiding explosives.

◊

Three years later, Salma, now at the age of forty-five, sounded paler and feebler than ever before. Stretching on her bed in a bundle of shawls, she was striving to picture the vague vision of her son whom she saw for the last time six years ago. Sweat was mingled with a few tears and trickling down her cheeks. While she was reenacting in her mind the last moments she spent with her son, she recalled his promise that he would come back. Another tear made its way down her cheek. The poor mother felt her heart drop again when she heard a sound echo loudly in her mind, the sound that penetrated her ears for three years. It was the sound which bore her the news of her son's death. The last tear had come to a halt at her lips. Her lips curled. The tear dropped off.

On a Drop of Rain

by Refaat Alareer

SCIENTISTS STILL DO NOT UNANIMOUSLY AGREE WHETHER RAIN-drops originate in the sky as ice crystals or not. But that does not matter to me. I am no scientist.

Abu Samy is a Palestinian farmer from the West Bank. He was busy on that windy day weeding his field—or what was left of it. He regretted not listening to his wife's frequent pleas not to go out. He was always doubtful about what she calls her "special gift," her "sense of the rain." He never listened to her, and if he did, he did not pay attention to her interpretations and elaboration of her different methods of skillfully and accurately predicting when it will or will not rain, for how long, and how heavy the rain will be. Although she must have told him the very same tale hundreds of times, he cannot retell her explanation except in excerpts. Um Samy touches the earth. She holds a tiny grain of sand, whispers to it, and listens back. In cases when communication fails, she smells the grain. But that is metaphorically speaking. At least Abu Samy thinks so.

On the southern side of the Wall, Abu Samy, along with thousands of Palestinian farmers, is not allowed to build rooms or erect tents, lest they should use these tents or structures to dig tunnels to the Israeli side. At least Abu Samy is luckier than his fellow farmers; he lost only two thirds of his land. Countless others of his friends and relatives had their fields swallowed by the Israeli Wall cutting through the lands of the West Bank. For Abu Samy at this very moment, the wall was useful. Living under occupation has taught him to see hope in the darkest of tunnels—not that he digs such tunnels to infiltrate into the Israeli side. He ran to the Wall. Gluing himself to the lengthy expanse of concrete, he was shielded from the heavy rain and the strong wind, though only partially, by the Wall.

On the other side of the Wall stood an Israeli farmer whose wife, too, had predicted rain (and warned him against Palestinians infiltrating the security fence). He wanted to run to the concrete room he built a couple of weeks ago, but as the Wall was closer, he hurried toward it. If they both had listened carefully, Abu Samy and the Israeli farmer would have heard their hearts beating against the Wall. Or maybe they did hear the heartbeats but mistook them for the rumble of distant thunder.

It was one particular drop of rain, a very tiny one. It could have fallen on Abu Samy's bare head had it not been for a sudden gust of wind that pushed it to the other side of the Wall; it fell on the Israeli farmer's helmet. He never felt it.

Other drops, however, were racing toward and seemingly preferring the unshielded head of Abu Samy.

That drops of rain begin their existence as ice crystals seems, to Abu Samy, very possible. But who cares about Abu Samy's views. He is Palestinian.

Please Shoot to Kill

by Jehan Alfarra

"I DON'T KNOW WHETHER I SHOULD BLAME ISRAEL OR MYSELF for not printing out my assignment," Laila grumbled in anguish. "Perhaps I should even blame my uncle for forgetting to bring some fuel for the power generator!" Her pace quickened as she stalked back and forth across her room, worry creeping into her mind. "How naïve of me to trust the electricity schedule and not see it coming. I should have known that having electricity for two days in a row was not some rare kindness on their part. I should have known that Israel would make me pay a great price!" A sense of resignation and foreboding began to settle over her thoughts as she condemned herself to the fact that her failure was inevitable. "I can't believe I actually waited until the night of the midterm to print my work and didn't consider that the electricity might go out and stay out, even though it was supposed to be back on at 3 p.m. today!"

She was sitting there in the dark; her little sister, Salma, who was five years old, was lying on the mattress next to her, and Sarah, who just celebrated her twelfth birthday, was fast asleep. Hardly able to hear herself think with the aggravating, annoying noise of the neighboring generator, she tried to skim through the pages on her laptop, although mostly she was just watching the low battery indicator almost hit zero. And...there it goes.... The flashes of the red X on the indicator laid down the law.

She crossed over to the bedroom window in dismay and leaned over it, and placing her forearms on top of each other, she gazed into the horizon. The sky merged, so strangely and beautifully, with the ground, forming one black surface patterned with an array of white dots, much like polka dots, which she loved so much. It always amazed her to see how those buildings on the other side of the border in the distance, with their windows always lit, appeared as an extension of the starry sky.

A sigh left her lips as she turned around and crossed over to the drawer of her dresser where she kept the candles, and placing a candle on her dresser, she drew the lighter from her pocket. The soft flame sprang up, passing from the lighter to the candle wick. She mysteriously found comfort and contentment in the burning beauty of this candle, a feeling that never grew old. She could sit for hours just watching the flame blaze on and burn out, occasionally playing with the wax with the tips of her fingers.

A reflection loomed in the mirror behind the candle—a scarred forehead, two cavernous hazel eyes, a nose, and slightly parted lips. She smiled and her eyes twinkled, and she watched how the reflection smiled exactly the same. She gestured to the reflection with her finger and, sneering, she uttered, "You will suck at your exam tomorrow, Laila," though the reflection did not reply. Her smile soon dimmed; another sigh made its way out of her dry lips, to be dampened by an intense tear trickling down her face. Her hand moved up swiftly to wipe it off, as though it were a sin for her to cry. She must not cry. She hated that. But how could she not? Two years passed now since the war. And she...well, she had been strong all along.

The memory of her father replayed and replayed in her head like a never-ending wheel, making her wonder if she should drop her medical degree altogether. The mere thought that she might have to do what those doctors were forced to do with him haunted her. "I will be cursed. I will be blamed. And I will be helpless, yet responsible for people's lives!" she thought to herself, rubbing both eyes with her cold fingers, "Maybe I should quit medical school. Will I ever be strong enough for it, to keep up with it? It's been two years now. Two bloody years."

◊

It was an oddly quiet night. She had finally fallen asleep at the break of dawn, crammed with her two sisters on the floor of their dim living room, wrapped up in a couple of sheets, with only the sound of silence filling the space. They had been desperately trying to pass the time they had lost track of, trying to escape the uncertainty of reality and the hideousness of the past two weeks, which had been nothing but a series of very appalling days and altogether horrendous nights—fifteen nights of immense horror and fear that one of those loaded Apaches flying over their house non-stop, or one of those blood-thirsty, monster-like Merkava tanks outside might be bombarding their house instead of their neighbors'. Fifteen nights of barely any electricity, any phone lines, or any food. Her father, numbed by the intimidation of bullets that had caused more than a few holes in their house and frozen by his inability to ensure the safety of his beloved wife and children, was leaning against the wall of their living room, with his hands in his pockets, his gray eyes watching them breathe slowly as they slept. He looked at his wife, who was fearfully reclining next to them, desperately trying to comfort her little one with a bedtime story, not being able, just like him, to do anything to stop those soldiers from harassing them anytime they felt like it. It was then when four Israeli soldiers broke into their house, kicking the door down with their boots, and holding M16 rifles in their hands.

Her mother jumped in shock, one hand pressing tightly around her three-year-old Salma, who went on crying, and the other covering her mouth so as not to utter a sound. Her heart skipped a beat. The fear locked up any utterance in her throat and any tears in her eyes. Laila's father did not know if it was wise for him to approach his young ones and beloved wife. It was risky with such unpredictable creatures in their house, he thought. To stay still might be safer. All he could do was stand there and pray that they would leave them alone. Laila knew it would be an inconceivable folly to look them in the eye, but the rage in her heart could not take it. She stared and stared at that one soldier until he fixed his two eyes on her, pointing his gun towards her, and she, without even a blink, did not look away. He then shifted his gun towards her father, with a smirk like that of a senseless crocodile. He held it there for a few seconds that were the longest and most torturous in the family's entire history. He did not fire at him. Not yet. Rather, he approached him until he was only twenty centimeters away. He grabbed Abu Laila's hair from the back, sinking his untrimmed nails in his scalp, and forced him on his knees.

All the while, the rest of the soldiers were roaming about the room, chatting in Hebrew, one of them picking the pictures off the walls and ransacking the place, and another fiddling with the school books and notes of the younger ones. Nothing could stop them from terrorizing everyone—not the sobbing of Laila and her mother, and certainly not the wailing of the little girls. Her father could not raise his eyes, not fearing for himself as much as fearing for his family. The soldier started speaking to him in Hebrew. The father understood some Hebrew but could not speak it. He did not respond. The soldier started kicking him on his bent knees, and with the edge of his gun, he hit him repeatedly in the stomach. The pain was immense. Her father took it in soundlessly, for his family. The last strike to his chest was so devastating that Abu Laila fell down instantly squirming and squealing in pain. Everyone watched in horror as guns were pointed at their heads. Laila could not tell whether taking action would worsen the already bad situation. The echoes of the soldiers' laughs filled the air of the living room. The soldiers walked toward the door, but before they left, a soldier wanted to finalize his job. He shouted, *"Arab mekhabel!"*—Arab terrorist!—spat on the floor of the room, aimed his gun at the struggling father, and...bang! A shot was fired.

Um Laila let out her long-suppressed scream, and she, Laila, and little Sarah crawled over to Abu Laila, who had already passed out. Amidst the cries and the excruciating event, her mother forgot three-year-old Salma where she was lying down, and in a split second, they heard a ravaging explosion that shook them inside out. The room was covered in black patches of smoke that blew in from the broken windows. Little Salma was hit.

Laila, Um Laila, and little Sarah found themselves forced to be paramedics. Laila leaped to pick up Salma in her hands and place her in her mother's lap. Salma's leg was dangling, swinging from what remained of her sinews, muscle, and tendons. Blood gushed forth as though from a nightmarish spring. Um Laila did not know whether to hold her daughter or her husband.

The sounds of ambulances could soon be heard in the distance, and unhesitatingly, Laila ran towards the door. Her Mom, shouting at her, cried even louder, unable to hold her breath or conceal her pain, "Stay here! Lailaaa...Laila...my dear, *habibti*, don't do this to me. This is more than enough.... Come back. I beg you...." Um Laila cried and cried, and Sarah joined her weeping mother.

Laila, determined to get help, stood at what was left of the door, one hand wiping her tears and the other pressing against her heart, not allowing her knees to let her down. She tried to sneak a quick look at what was going on outside. It was cold, dark, and rainy. She could spot three tanks standing in the distance, like ghosts of the most horrifying type. She could hear an ambulance, though there was no sight of any. An Apache flew over the house, forcing Laila down on her knees. Soon, the drones came to accompany them, making the sounds of the night even creepier. Laila had to pick herself up. She had to save her father and she had to save her sister. Three more bombs rocked the area, one falling in the small piece of land they lived off of, shaking the ground and throwing Laila ferociously back into the house, where she fell down motionless, blood seeping through her nose and ears, and down her face, mingling with her tears. Numbness overcame her fragile body. She felt nothing and heard nothing.

◊

Laila opened her blurry eyes to find herself in a jam-packed room of five beds, where others were lying, surrounded by their families and a few doctors rushing about. She looked around for someone to recognize and noticed Sarah, clutching at the hospital bed sheet like she used to hold her teddy bear as she slept, sleeping at the end of the bed. Laila could feel something on her face—a bandage. She tried to remember what had happened. She murmured, forcing the words out, "Baba...Salma...." Sarah woke up to Laila's words and slight stirring. She held her hand and said, "Mama is with them. Don't worry; they are fine." Laila fell back asleep.

Sarah let go of Laila's hand and walked out of the room. The corridor was full to capacity with people lying here and there; she could hardly find space to move her feet. Some were sleeping on the floor, some were crying and some were moaning; it was all too much for her to see. She found a little corner next to a door and curled up there, pulling her legs towards her and placing her forehead on her knees. She had already cried enough that no more tears were left to be shed. She could not bear staying with her family. It was too much for her little heart. Sarah did not know why it all happened. All she knew is that it meant Apaches, F16s, tanks, bullets, soldiers, and blood.

Abu Laila and Salma survived. Salma was too young to realize she will probably never walk again. Abu Laila, on the other hand, had a ripped kidney from the bullet, which pierced right through, and a broken chest bone from the blows of the butt of the rifle. Fatty droplets—tiny particles of fat from the area of the bone fracture—got into his bloodstream and passed through the heart to his lungs. The droplets triggered immune mechanisms in the lungs, filling the lungs with fluid and blocking the ability to take in oxygen, resulting in lung hemorrhage.

The family stayed in the hospital for three days, Abu Laila on a ventilator until the doctors had finally managed to stabilize him. They could not stay at the hospital any longer. The offensive was still in full swing, the hospital was receiving more and more bodies of dead and injured people, and there was a severe lack of space. Many injured people had to leave prematurely to make space for others.

The radio was the only means for them to know what was going on up north in Beit Hanoun, where the family lived, and apparently, the invasion of their area was still well underway; it was unsafe for them to go back. Not that the hospital, which got its own share of the bombardment, was safe either. It was, however, relatively safer than any other place in the locked-down Gaza Strip. Um Laila called her sister, Mona, who lived in the middle of Gaza City to stay with them.

After she hung up, she went up to the doctor, her heavy heart hurting and little Sarah holding onto her hand tightly, and told him they had found a place to stay. The doctor gave her a few glucose drips, and instructed her and Laila how to use them. He had also warned her of some life-threatening complications and said that Abu Laila needed to be taken back to the hospital once the situation had settled down. Nobody knew when that would be.

Amidst the bombing and intimidation of the Israeli jets, the family managed to reach Mona's home. Five days had passed, in fear, pain, and torment. But then, the next morning came, and it was too quiet, something they found dreadful, for it usually meant the worst was yet to come. However, this time it was the end of the offensive. The shelling and killing stopped.

For Laila's family though, the greater suffering had just started.

As the family headed back to their home, they found that their plot of land had become nothing more than a pile of debris. The entire harvest of the year was gone, though they had no choice but to make do with what they had and to fix what could be fixed. After all, it was not the first time Abu Laila had his land shelled or bulldozed. But this time, Abu Laila could not start over. His health was severely damaged. He needed to have a kidney operation in Cairo. It could not be conducted in Gaza, nor could the lung hemorrhage be treated efficiently without the necessary equipment that Gaza hospitals lack. Abu Laila's case was indeed critical. Nonetheless, his case was not rated as critical as those of hundreds of other injured people, and consequently he was not allowed to travel outside Gaza for medical treatment.

Laila could see her Dad's pain was not just physical. His pain was the pain of his family. It was in the thought of him being a burden rather than a breadwinner at a time they needed him the most. Laila was torn between running from this hospital to that, working on her father's papers, and studying for her secondary school *tawjihi* exams to win the scholarship she had always dreamed of. Um Laila was torn between taking care of her injured husband and daughter, and running their farm. And Sarah, once a cheeky little girl, was trapped in the images of death and destruction, and the feelings of fear, pain, rage, and hatred. Sarah will never get therapy. She will, however, continue to look after little Salma and play with her, and will continue to sleep next to her father, whose tears became his nightly ritual.

Abu Laila's condition was deteriorating day by day. Four months of agony had passed when, one day, Laila picked up the phone to hear the voice of the doctor telling her that, by the end of the week, they will have sent Abu Laila's file and that he might have a chance of traveling for the surgery. It was the first good news in a long time. Laila could not believe her ears, nor could her mother believe her. "Are you sure he said this? Laila, are you positive? When will they send it? When will we get the reply?" asked Um Laila with the tears of joy rushing uncontrollably down her face.

They could not wait until the end of the week. Those five days went by so slowly that their hearts were racing non-stop and their minds knew no sleep. Finally, he will be going out for treatment. Finally, he will be able to go back to work. He will be able to eat properly, to take them out, to laugh from the very depth of his heart, and he will not have to constantly worry that he might be dying. Finally, Laila will be able to study without worrying constantly, and Sarah will not have to see her father cry quietly or hear her parents talk about death and future possibilities anymore. And little Salma will be getting all the attention and care of the entire family.

Thursday had come. At last. The clock struck 6 a.m., and Laila and her mother were already up. They made breakfast for the family, got dressed, and headed to the hospital right away. They could not wait for the phone call. They wanted to go and see for themselves.

They arrived at the reception and asked to see Dr. Mahmoud. He wasn't there just yet. The two hours of waiting seemed to Laila and her mother longer than the five days. The minute the doctor walked in, Um Laila jumped from her seat and called in anticipation, "Dr. Mahmoud!" Fixing his glasses and swallowing his words, Dr. Mahmoud replied, "Oh. Um Laila...."

His facial expressions and his words were not very encouraging. The sight of him with that face made Laila and her mother shudder. It gave them a silent yet painful pinch in the heart. Should they go on and ask him about the papers? Or do they not want to hear something that might upset them and crush the beautiful fantasies of the past five days, something that might absolutely destroy any last bit of hope they had? Every bit of his face was saying, "Don't ask about the papers. Don't ask about the file. Don't ask about the Goddamn treatment!" They did not ask. Neither Laila nor her mother could utter a single word. Dr. Mahmoud cut to the chase and said, "Um Laila, look.... Your husband is quite critical. If you were in my position, would you send his file or the file of a dying baby who has a better chance of recovery?"

A few tears that were struggling to roll down Um Laila's face choked back any words or questions she might have had.

He went on, "We had a baby come in this week who has a serious blood condition, and if he does not travel for treatment as soon as possible, the little one might pass away before he even learns how to walk. And due to the circumstances, we only can send one person."

Um Laila gasped in shock as to what this might entail, as Laila shouted intensely, "Who are you to choose who lives or dies?!" Despite her yelling, Dr. Mahmoud continued steadily, "Look, I am terribly sorry. There is nothing we can do about this. We only do what we can, and if anything comes up, I will make sure to call you. I have to go now. I have a patient waiting. Take care of yourself Um Laila, of your daughters, and of your husband. God bless you."

Everything just stopped. Only waiting remained. And this time it was waiting for the worst. Everything seemed insignificant. Time was insignificant, pain was insignificant, hope was insignificant, fear was insignificant, and the lives of people were definitely the most insignificant of all.

Laila wanted to shout, to scream her heart out. But she couldn't. Her mother was having it bad enough. Laila must be strong for her now. One woman crying and howling in the middle of the reception room was more than enough. Her mother had a nervous breakdown. What were they going to tell Abu Laila now? What were they going to tell the man who a short while ago was setting plans for what he would do for his family once he was healthy again? Nothing. Simply nothing.

Abu Laila died three months later.

Regardless of the anguish, Laila tried to convince herself and her family that they were still "fortunate" compared to others. The family was lucky that the walls of their house were still standing, and they did not have to live in a tent and endure the brutality of winter's cold and summer's heat. Salma, who was still in diapers when she got hit by an Israeli missile, was also lucky that her brain was still in its place, that she was able to get treatment inside Gaza, and that the roof of the house did not fall on her body, forcing the family to dig up the pieces of her flesh from underneath. Um Laila was lucky her physical health was good, and that she was able to fend for her family and provide for them. Sarah was lucky she was not also physically injured, adding to her psychological disturbance. And Laila was also lucky to pass out and not witness more of what could only be called hell on earth, before they were taken to the hospital. She was also lucky she had the ability to still concentrate enough to ace her exams and win the scholarship she had always dreamed of. The family's calamity was not that much of a calamity when placing it on the scale of severity of Gaza's tragedies.

Laila did not hate the little baby whose file was sent instead of her father's. She only hated Israel for making it so that the doctor had to choose. She only wished this baby would survive, grow up, and become a freedom fighter. "No, I can't drop medical school. Not after all that has happened," she said under her breath. Laila sat in her bedroom, the candle burning out, and as she heard the sound of an Israeli Apache ripping through the sky, she looked over, and in that weak moment and in the memory of all the suffering following her father's injury, she muttered through clenched teeth, "Next time, finish your job. When you bomb, bomb to end. And when you shoot, please shoot to kill."

Omar X

by Yousef Aljamal

THE NIGHT WAS SILENT. THE MOON HID BEHIND SOME SUMMER clouds. His smile revealed his young age. His steps beat the ground slowly, looking for the path. The thump-thump sound of a helicopter was getting closer, penetrating the peace of the crowded refugee camp his family had lived in since 1948, and the familiar noise of tanks rolling in violated the silence of the night and decreed that he will never sleep again. He got into his khaki uniform hastily, grabbed his gun, and rubbing its dusty barrel, stormed out of the house. As he waited a little at the doorstep of their house to make sure no one was watching, his eyes wandered right and left, and finally met the eyes of his friend, who was murdered three months ago and is now immortalized in posters stuck on walls of the camp. Those honey eyes of his best friend always brought him comfort. As the helicopter moved away for a while, silence prevailed again.

Soon after, Sa'ad joined him, and together they entered an orange orchard. Sa'ad insisted on going in first. Omar followed after Sa'ad made sure no soldiers were around. "The place must be safe. Let's get closer to that building in the middle. We can see things clearer from there," Omar suggested in a whisper.

The grass under their feet was fresh; the only noise they could hear was that of the branches rubbing against them as they went further. Sa'ad stopped to check his gun. Omar did the same. They stood still for a second. Silence was heard again, this time even clearer. It all made sense now. That silence was artificial. Omar and Sa'ad did not have time to communicate, except for some glances. Bullets poured from the building into them. Omar fell down, shot. "Watch out! Crawl on the ground!" Sa'ad, still in disbelief, shouted. More bullets whizzed by.

Omar's life flashed quickly in front of his eyes. He saw himself as a child, being spoiled by his dad. He saw himself as a student, throwing his little pocket money in protest, the coins scattering on the roof of their rusty house. He saw himself leading protests as his young companions got killed. He saw himself as a singer, singing for freedom. Lastly, he saw himself as a fighter.

The dusty, narrow corridor which led to the maternity ward was full of relatives wearing full-cheeked smiles coming to congratulate his parents. Months before his birth, during a family gathering, his name was declared, while their refugee camp was under curfew. "Father, my oldest brother named his first son after you, Ibrahim. It's not proper at all to have the same name as my brother, Abu Ibrahim. I am going to name him Omar. This name reminds me of kindness and toughness at the same time," Abu Omar declared. His grandfather was satisfied with the name, even though Omar wasn't named after him, as the tradition usually goes. His mother showed no resistance to her husband's zeal for the name. When the boy was born, he was taken to be washed by none other than his grandmother, as that was tradition, too.

"To Palestine, I grant you. I want to see you a handsome man. Avoid the Israeli soldiers on your way. Fight them back, if they hurt you. Long live my little child," Omar's dad sang as he fell asleep upon his arrival from an unplanned trip to the occupied territories.

The curfew was in place when his mother and her newborn boy tried to sneak under the cover of the night to their tin house in the refugee camp. Five soldiers stopped their car for a regular check and allowed them to continue driving toward the entrance of the neighborhood, named Block A after a British prison that was built there in the 1940s. An Israeli soldier, who looked like none of the refugees there, stood at the checkpoint, looking at the mother bringing one more child to the area, which was well-known for children throwing stones, rocks, and whatever they found at the soldiers. "What do you have in your lap?" the solider asked. "*Yilid*," Um Omar said, using the Hebrew word for "child." The driver grabbed a cigarette and left the sound of Fairouz singing, "We will return someday to our neighborhood," for the soldiers to listen to.

A second bullet hit Omar's body.

"You almost suffocate him as your lips tour every inch of his little face. He's crying. Please, stop kissing him that way," Um Omar would protest. "My love for him is immeasurable. It gets bigger every day, but it never gets old," Abu Omar said in defense of his embraces.

During a full moon, that night silent, too, the soldiers stormed Omar's bedroom, looking for some kids who were throwing stones at them, spoiling Omar's imagining the moon as a white balloon. Um Omar hugged her son to hide him from the red eyes of the soldiers invading every corner of the room. Omar's mother never imagined him as a fighter. She abhorred guns now even more. "My little son, sleep. My loved one, sleep," she sang to comfort him during his terrifying childhood.

Faster than the wind, which blew very often with the smell of gunpowder, Omar grew up in a rusty house that got narrower as his extended family doubled. Omar realized that the soldiers, who used to scare him as a five-year-old boy on his way to kindergarten, still invaded every little aspect of his life.

Omar's astonishing voice helped him meet many people while performing resistance songs, including some young men who happened to be fighters. He decided to join them to protect the camp from the continuous raids.

A third and last bullet broke the scary silence, easily making it to Omar's body.

"Mom, I am serious about it. I want money to buy an AK-47 to fight those soldiers. They kill children and women. It's my duty," Omar demanded.

Despite her love for her first son, Omar's mother could do nothing to stop him. She wanted him to study hard to pass his high school final exams. "Just study hard this year, then you can put off your education for a few years," Um Omar suggested, urging him to focus on his school. "I will bring you a certificate that will make you raise your head proudly high in the sky," Omar would say to comfort his increasingly worried mother.

As he bled, a song he loved and always sang jumped to his mind: "My mother prepared me a comfortable bed. She made me a leather pillow and wished me eternal happiness. This is your bride, shining like a diamond...."

Omar was too fragile to take out his mobile and make a last call to his family. He kept bleeding, and the bullets kept coming. He swung his head to his right. Face down, Sa'ad was lying lifeless next to him. He gathered enough strength and extended his hand over Sa'ad's body. And before he could do anything, his hand fell down.

We Shall Return

by Mohammed Suliman

ABU IBRAHIM DRAGGED HIS FEET AS HIS WEAK BODY STRUGGLED with the bundle on his shoulders. His body staggered. His feet tirelessly tried to carry him as far as they could, and though they failed to keep his body stable, he didn't fall. Abu Ibrahim wasn't alone. He had a long line of followers; they were his family. He was accompanied by his two wives and a dozen of his children aged five to twenty-two years old. Abu Ibrahim was leaving, but he didn't know where he was going. There were hundreds of people around him, and everybody was doing the same. Everybody was leaving. And all of them didn't know where they were going. There was Abu Ahmed with his wife, his two married sons walking on either side of him, another two unmarried sons, and four daughters, followed by a line no less than that which was following Abu Ibrahim. They were leaving, too. There was Abu Naser and his kin, who made some twenty in number following him in one line. Weary with the loads they had to carry, all of them were leaving. Where, they didn't know.

Amidst the growing, thick dust that rose from the shuffling feet of the leavers which strove to keep their owners standing upright, nothing was audible but the chaotic sounds of the shoes scraping the rough, rocky sands and, every now and then, stumbling upon a stone. Scores and scores of people were roaming around, all of them stooping down with the burdens on their shoulders and backs. Not knowing where they were going, they walked and walked on. The only thing they knew was that it was a black day, for someone had come and made them leave their homes, farms, and olive trees, and as they said "no," a gun was pointed at their faces to make them leave, so they left in the hope that they will come back again. How, they did not know.

It was the Nakba. And since then, they moved two or three times to different destinations, having to endure saying "no" to their offspring who asked, "Are we going back?" Their bundles were getting bigger and heavier, and the roads did not seem to unravel their own village. The sun had just fallen when Abu Ibrahim, Abu Ahmed, and Abu Naser gathered around a small fire to discuss their hazy destiny. Their families sat peacefully under the wide, starry sky, the wind gusting through the trees and the tents they set up out of their rags. The chaotic trudging had vanished as the sun fell. It was replaced with the dreadful sound of silence, the crackling fire, and the wind that occasionally whistled. As the wind blew, the crackling of the fire grew more dreadful, interrupted by the giggles of the little children who squirmed as their mother tickled their armpits and forced a laugh out of their chests.

Abu Ibrahim aptly started a conversation with a deep sigh that might have been confused with a moan of an Arabian mare, alone in the bosom of night, crying over the sudden death of her little colt. Indeed, it was a moan of an Arab, whose father had taught him how to be as proud as the sun even before he could write down his own name, and whose pride had been wounded.

"Be'een Allah, ya Abu Ibrahim,"—God's going to help us, Abu Ibrahim—said Abu Naser, immediate replying to his neighbor's distressed sigh as he aimlessly drew circles in the sand before silence fell again.

"God will help us," came the voice of Abu Ahmed, who skillfully tickled his rosary. "I think the Arabs, especially the

Egyptian government, won't keep silent," he said. "They will do something to get us back to our homes."

"Yes," his counterpart nodded approvingly.

"And don't forget there are our brothers, the Saudis," said Abu Ahmed. Noticing the approving nods of Abu Naser, he gradually raised his voice as he went on. "And the Jordanians, the Syrians, and the Iraqis, and the Algerians and all our Arab brothers. All of them will rush to our help and fight these brutes out of our country."

"Yes, they will!" Plucking up his courage and feeling the enthusiasm of his neighbor's tone, Abu Naser ceased nodding to take part in this passionate speech. "They will crush these animals and kick them out of here!"

While Abu Naser delivered his portion of this confident, morale-boosting speech, Abu Ahmed, all of a sudden, looked sullen again, as though he had changed his mind about the Arabs within this very short period of time. That being the case, he, to Abu Naser's disappointment, didn't say anything. He waited and waited, but Abu Ahmed said nothing.

It all ended here, and silence reigned over the fire-lit session again.

After this brief break of silence, Abu Ahmed started again, however, this time, in a voice so calm, low, and hesitant, his eyes fixed on the scribbles his twig drew on the sand and never meeting those of the others. "Yes, maybe they will, but we don't know how long that's going to take." He looked as though he was talking to himself rather than to his companions, "It might take one week, two, one month, two months, and even half a year. Who knows?"

"Fal Allah wala falak ya zalame,"—God forbid!—Abu Ibrahim suddenly spoke out. "What are you saying? Half a year? Do you think we'll stay in these tents for half a year? No, no, no. I don't think so," Abu Ibrahim continued, widening his eyes in furious amazement as he spoke.

At this moment, both Abu Naser and Abu Ahmed wanted to say something. They exchanged looks for a while, as each of them waited for the other to say what he wanted to say. Each opened his mouth, started, hesitated, paused, and at the end, both remained silent. No one spoke up. No one had enough courage to say they realized what would later be a fact. Neither wanted to tell Abu Ibrahim—or rather to remind him—that it might take a little while longer than half a year before they could return to their homes, lands, farms, and olive trees. And it all ended there.

Meanwhile, steadying a broken pottery jug of water in her right hand while balancing it on her head, Um Ibrahim in her embroidered black dress, decorated with an intense, raised, red pattern and her child, bare-footed, hurrying after her, came jogging up to her husband, and said, *"Ayzeen 'amalko shay?"*—Do you want me to make you some tea?

"Yes, make some tea. Why not?" Abu Ibrahim replied. He had now joined his two neighbors drawing circles on the sand.

The three men kept quiet as they carried on their relaxing activity. It was relieving, indeed, for the twigs, tightly pressed in the farmers' fists, had now been fully implanted in the sands. It must have comforted them to plant a twig in the sands. Only then, Abu Ibrahim felt his growing uneasiness as silence extended before him, and feeling inclined to break this silence, he started improvising a hymn: *"Raj'een ya blady"*—We shall return, oh, Homeland—only to be joined by Abu Ahmed, who repeated after Abu Ibrahim in a slightly higher tone. Abu Naser, feeling the rising, passionate tone of this song, couldn't help but raise his voice and take part in the singing.

"We shall return, Homeland, we shall return."

Now, it being all three of them singing, the song went awkwardly. No harmony dominated as everyone sang on his own, and each willing to maintain his own rhythm over the other's, it looked as though each was cutting in on the other, rather than singing with him.

"Oh w ba'den ya jama'a"—Okay, what then, people?—Abu Ibrahim started angrily. "Are you going to keep bleating like this?"

"Ok, let's start all over again," Abu Ahmed replied.

"Mashi"—Okay—Abu Naser said.

"One rhythm, one tone, don't forget," Abu Ibrahim reminded them. *"Wahad tneeeeen talata"*—One, twoooo, three.

Raj'eenlek ya bladee, raj'eenlek rajeen—We shall return to you, oh, Homeland. We shall return.

Raj'een la qaryetnah, raj'een la hakoretna—We shall return to our village. We shall return to our field.

Raj'een ya zaytonah, raj'een ya laymonah—We shall return, oh, olive tree. We shall return, oh, lemon tree.

They started altogether, keeping the same rhythm and the same tone they had wished for, Abu Ibrahim leading them to teach them the tone and the words he improvised. Hardly had a few moments passed when Abu Ibrahim was indignantly rebuking his two neighbors for failing again to sing in harmony.

"Let's try again," he said.

The three men carried on their efforts trying to sing in harmony, but they failed to maintain it for more than a few moments each time they tried. They tried time and again until they reached their sixty-fifth attempt, and yet never did they succeed in uniting their voice. They were truly bleating. And at a long last, exhausted with the long distance he had crossed and seeing the futility of his painstaking efforts to keep up with the other two men, Abu Naser just fell asleep, and soon after, he was followed by Abu Ahmed and Abu Ibrahim. The fire had died, and, every now and then, a cold, gentle breeze blew over the half-standing tents. Everyone had fallen asleep.

In the morning, the three men, Abu Ibrahim, Abu Ahmed, and Abu Naser, stooped down as they walked on, struggling with the burden over their shoulders and followed by their sons, daughters, wives, and hundreds of people here and there, all doing the same thing. All were leaving.

From Beneath

by Rawan Yaghi

I DIDN'T EVEN KNOW IF MY EYES WERE OPEN.

After the chaos, everything seemed so calm. I sensed the dust covering my face. It seemed to block my nostrils, and as I tried to inhale through them, I felt I made it worse. I decided to breathe through my lips. I could feel my breath hitting one of the bricks. I heard a faint shout of an ambulance siren and then my breath was the only sound I could hear. One of my arms was trapped somewhere under the wooden edges of my bed, the other under what seemed like more heavy bricks. My toes, my legs, and my hair were jailed and sentenced not to move. I felt a lot of pain, but I couldn't figure out where it was coming from. I was never trapped in so little a space. My world felt so narrow and sharp.

I was afraid. I waited and waited and, as my mother once advised me to do when I was afraid, I tried to recall all the joyful events in my life, though they were few: my older brother's big wedding party, my grandmother coming back from Mecca and bringing me a singing doll, the last *'eid* when I got my biggest *'eidiyya* ever, my mother bringing us home a new baby—though I wondered if that was a happy event for me, but I had certainly seen the joy my parents had looking at that little thing.

113

My breath softly came back to my face, with the smell of grayish objects rather than a breeze carrying the scent of our garden plants, touching my nose and cheeks as if to comfort and tell me that everything will be okay. But a minute later I started crying. The sky was starless. And only then did I realize that my eyes were closed, for I started to feel my sticky eyelashes. It did not matter, opening and closing them were thoroughly the same. I cried so much that my tears, mixed with the dust on my face, felt like mud crawling to the edges of my cheeks and filling the canals of my ears. I must have been bleeding, because a horrible pain started growing in my chest. The back of my head seemed to pull me down further and further with every scream I made, and I felt I had enough strength to push everything around me away. But nothing seemed to move. I desperately needed to stand up and run to my mother's warm hug. And just then it occurred to me. No one was coming to help me. There was no movement in any part of the house. I wept even harder.

I wanted to help. I tried to move. Only one muscle. A toe at a time. I felt something very sharp poking through my flesh.

I stopped crying. I waited. I bled.

Just Fifteen Minutes

by Wafaa Abu Al-Qomboz

"Mom, I want my dad. You must call him and tell him to come back home. Do you hear me?" Islam said, irritated.

"Islam, why are you yelling? Just wait a minute, and I will call him," she said.

"Okay, okay. I am sorry," Islam said. "I want to paint something. Dad always helps me; he is an excellent painter. My teacher asked all the students in the class to paint a map of their original villages," he explained to his mother. "I know that my country is the best, and my map will be fantastic. Dad told me this, when I started Grade 4," he continued.

Islam started to leave his room but hesitated for a bit. Something on the wall distracted his attention. He saw it almost every day, but he could not figure out what it was. This time he felt it was about to come to life, the trees swaying wildly, the clouds looming in the upper right corner. It was so vivid. He took some time to stare at the picture. It was a painting his father helped him paint, only this picture does not show the sun. He did not like that. He ran hastily to his mother.

"My dad, he is late...." Islam rushed back again to gaze at the picture on the wall. "Mom, Mom...I am talking to you. Can you hear me?" Islam shouted from the other room.

His mother, moving around the house normally, acted as if he was not speaking, as if he were not there at all.

"I remember when I was living there in that small house. It was a small house. The old tree, yes, which Dad planted. Yes, he planted it. Or maybe my grandfather did. No, I was the person who planted this tree," he yelled, hoping his mom would come and look.

Islam looked at his mother. He felt that she was so tired. He could see how her eyes were getting smaller and darker. He wished his father was there to help, but he spent most of his time outside their home. He did not seem to have time to help around the house, unless it was a heavy thing to lift. Islam wanted to be strong like him. Maybe he could help his mother, and then she would have time to speak to him instead of him talking to himself all the time. It was four o'clock and his father was not home yet. His mother once told him that his father was "wanted." He did not know what it meant except that he did not see much of his father.

"He must come before it gets dark," Islam hoped.

◊

"Islam...Islam, wake up!" a friendly, nasal voice called.

He turned his head to the place where the voice came from. He did not care.

◊

"Islam, Islam.... Your father will be here soon. He will stay for fifteen minutes this time. You know that your father is very busy, so be polite," came his mother's voice from the other room.

"Fifteen minutes? I can wait for fifteen minutes."

She smiled. "You are a naughty boy, aren't you?"

"But he is very late, and...." He smiled too and stared at the picture again.

"My map will be the best one. Dad will paint it for me. Well, I will help him a little. In addition, it is the map of my country and my house. It is my map. He makes me choose the colors (although I still remember how he once protested my use of red and suggested green instead) and sometimes allows me to color in. It is one of the few things I got to do with Dad, as he is a very busy person. Last time he promised to let me do all the coloring."

"Mooom, I tell you, I won't take the map with me to school if Dad does not show up as you say," he protested, hoping his father won't let him down. He wanted to take the map to school and show it around. He wanted to brag about it, about working together with his father to make it perfect.

◊

"Islam, Islam.... Wake up quickly. Argh, you're very lazy, man!" Joe snarled, hitting Islam with the two pillows on the sofa, his voice grating on Islam's nerves. "Islam, you will be very late; you know that you will be very late. If you don't wake up, I will have to...."

"No, please, just fifteen minutes. I know the Master's thesis. Anyway, please, just fifteen minutes. Don't pour water. It is so cold. Uh, you know, I like my tea with a little sugar. Please, let me sleep just for fifteen minutes. I need those fifteen minutes."

"I can wait fifteen minutes," Joe replied.

Islam stretched his hand calmly from beneath the pillow, gently touching the framed map next to his bed, making sure it was still there, and went back to sleep.

"You're finally home, Dad. You're finally home," he repeated in his sleep.

House

by Refaat Alareer

THEY STOOD STILL, ABSORBING EVERY LITTLE DETAIL OF THEIR house. They could not tell, despite Salem first being uncertain about his father's plan, if it was seeing their home again after three years that gave them both goosebumps.

The house was on a little hill overlooking olive and lemon groves that stretched westward, like a hand-woven green carpet extending endlessly and attached to the clear sky of the dawn with nothing but reddish threads of the early day. Their house was finally in front of them. These last steps leading to it, they realized, would be the most perilous, even deadly. Hope of return was their only motive, their only sustainer. Abu Salem hoped to get to his house; his son hoped they won't get shot at or, worse, arrested. Abu Salem carried a small, brown bag nearly the same color as his jacket. He refused to let his son carry it, despite his son's insistence.

The closer he got to the house, the more he sped up his pace, as if he were magnetically being pulled by the house. The two-story building still had the tent on the roof like it did three years ago. Abu Salem erected the tent soon after he moved to the house, lest he should forget the days his family spent in a tent in the Qalandia refugee camp. Forgetting, he believed, was a scandal, like surrendering to the enemy while you had plenty of ammunition; it was out of the question. Longing for that time when the only authority he had over him was that of his father, or that of his grandfather, became a daily ritual.

After what seemed like three hours of walking and crouching and hiding, they finally made it to their house. The last few hundred meters were the most difficult, though. The house was so close, yet so far away. As they neared the unfinished part of the Wall, they crawled, lay still for several minutes, and had to deal with several passing military patrol jeeps and stray dogs.

Abu Salem was a sixty-one-year-old refugee who taught English at his local village of Ni'lin in the West Bank. His oldest son, Salem, was accompanying him to go back to their house, which the occupation forcibly took exactly three years ago. As he aged under occupation, Abu Salem grew more and more obstinate. The occupation had taught him that. Teaching taught him to talk and to argue a lot. The occupation, his father, and his father's job as a teacher, all trained Salem to talk less and obey more.

Looking back, Salem felt sad he let his father go in the first place, though he had no choice but to obey his father this time, too. The idea of going back was absurd, even surreal. It bothered Salem sometimes how his father spoke about going back to their home, like when normal people under normal circumstances say they are going home from work or school. His father, Salem insisted, was oblivious to the facts on the ground: they simply can't go back—not now, not this way, not with all the security measures and the gigantic Wall snaking its way through their lives. Salem, of course was always careful to mention those reasons in those exact words. But so far, his father was right: their journey back was impossible because their thinking made it so. Once they were there, it would be possible. It was possible, but danger, for Salem, could be looming anywhere.

◊

"How?" Salem had asked when his father first told him he was going back and that he wanted Salem to come with him. But after all those years, he got used to his father's futile endeavors: his attempts to block the bulldozer that razed parts of his field, spending a lot of money on a lawsuit he filed to stop the confiscation of his house, his desperate search for someone to take his emotional missive to the Jewish family who might take the house in order to win their hearts, and now the trek up and down the mountainous fields to go back to have a final look at the house. All he wanted, he kept repeating to Salem, was one last look at the house he built himself and now could not even see because of the Wall.

"I already spoke to your mother about it, and she is fine as long as I take you with me," came the answer.

"How?" repeated Salem, through clenched teeth.

It was clear Abu Salem was reluctant to share the details with his son, but once he started to describe his plan, it was obvious he rehearsed the answer in his mind many times, as if he were preparing a difficult lesson plan.

Abu Salem explained how the last morning strolls he took were to check the best and least dangerous way and time, to familiarize himself with the geography of the road to be taken, and to talk to local shepherds for advice. He came to the conclusion that dawn was the best time. Salem was not sure it was a smile he saw drawn on his father's face soon after he revealed his plan, but Salem could swear his father's eyes twinkled. They only did that when Abu Salem's heart and mind were set on something.

"So we head towards the unfinished part of the Wall after midnight. We will reach before dawn. It will still be dark, and the patrol guards will be sleepy or too tired to be on the lookout." The words spilling out matter-of-factly, Abu Salem continued trying to avoid his son's quizzical looks.

"Are you going to hire a tracker?" Salem asked.

"I know how to go to my house. I do not need silly trackers," snapped Abu Salem.

◊

"We are close," mumbled Abu Salem as they approached their house, talking to himself rather than assuring Salem.

"Close to what? Dad, between us and our house stands death! These few hundred meters are always watched by the soldiers. I say we go back now before it is too late," argued Salem, finally finding some courage to voice his concerns when he realized that the situation was much worse than he expected.

"If you want to go back, just go. At least I will die trying," said the father decisively, hoping Salem would not go. Salem did not.

But apparently, Abu Salem's plan worked fine. The area was very quiet; they smoothly crossed to the other side of the Wall. And just when they felt relaxed, the acceleration of a passing army jeep brought them down to their knees.

They hid for a while behind a little pile of rubbish. Just before the jeep was out of sight, Abu Salem grabbed a branch, dragged it behind him, and sprinted towards the road to make use of the dust that lingered behind the jeep, beckoning to Salem, who could not figure out why his father did what he did, especially with the jeep still in the distance.

"Why didn't you grab a branch?" asked his father when Salem joined him, both clearly irritated.

"Why did you?" asked Salem.

"You should have dragged a branch to cover your footprints," Abu Salem snapped.

"Let's hope the dust and the wind will cover them up," replied Salem.

Their house and their trees gave them more safety now that they were a few meters away. Abu Salem spent the next five minutes examining the house and its surroundings. His facial expressions told there was something wrong. Salem was partly watching his father, partly looking at the house, and partly making sure no one else was nearby.

"Occupation is rude and thoughtless. But I have never heard of any occupation more inconsiderate and tactless than this. Unless they're doing this on purpose to torture us, there is something seriously wrong with their minds. Sick!" Abu Salem burst out.

Looking at his Dad, Salem was unable to determine the cause of the outburst. "What's wrong?" he asked.

"What's wrong? Nothing is wrong! That's what's wrong!"

Salem, who was not in the mood for another of his father's temper tantrums, opened his mouth to ask again, but no words came out.

"The only thing that kept me from coming back here all these years is the fear I might not recognize my own house. But there is no sign of obliteration. The house stands there just like it did three years ago. They just come to your house or farm and kick you out. And it's theirs. Look at those olive groves. They let the farmers toil all year long, and then they come heavily armed at the end of the year and pick—steal!—the olives. It's like they're no more depending solely on their total military superiority, but they also love to slap us and to humiliate us. It's like they're saying, 'We take what belongs to you. So what? What can you do about it?'" Abu Salem stopped to take a breath. "Today I swear I'll show them what we are capable of," he added. "If they're mocking us, today I'll make fun of their pride, their security."

Salem never thought of the issue that way. His father always came up with subtle interpretations to things people do or say, that Salem developed the habit of doubting what those people really meant. But this time, it was his father's promise to "show them" that mesmerized him.

"I'll be out in fifteen minutes." Abu Salem instructed his son to wait outside and be on the lookout, and squeezed himself through the hole the army made the night his house was raided.

Salem spent the next ten minutes fretting, his father's oath eating him up. And then against his father's advice, he too squeezed himself in. What Salem saw was something he would not have imagined, not even in his wildest dreams.

There were wires—lots of them—small tubes, a timer, and two small mobile phones. Apparently those were the contents of the bag. "Dad! What is this?!" he exclaimed.

"It's a bomb," replied his father, as if replying to someone asking for the time.

"Is that what you carried all the way in your bag? I don't understand! What do you want to do?" asked Salem.

"I want to destroy the house," replied his father. "If I can't have it, no one else should."

"You're going to kill us! This is suicide! Madness! Destroy the house?! Your own house?! What will people say? That you destroyed your own house?" Salem started firing questions, not sure which will make his father change his mind.

"Yes," answered Abu Salem—maybe the toughest "yes" he had ever uttered.

"But, Dad, it is your house no matter who has it. It is temporary. Sooner or later it will be yours again," argued Salem forcefully.

"Listen, son, it depends on how you word it for people. I am destroying what was taken from me, by force, without my consent. And I am doing this when all other means failed. Perhaps I was wrong from the beginning. I should've destroyed the house the first day Israel decided to confiscate it. All these courts, lawsuits, and hearings allowed by the occupation are fake formalities. Now I can't just simply let them take it away, can I?" argued the father, caring very little whether that made much sense.

"But it's your house. Your own house! How could you do that?" Salem asked entirely bewildered.

"Salem, my ability to make sound judgment has been compromised, I know. Having choices under occupation has long become a thing worse, much worse, than being deprived of choices altogether. They oblige us to choose between two good options or two bad ones. In both cases, we are to suffer and to sacrifice. We then have to live with the nightmares of choosing one over the other. We hate the occupation for that more than we hate it for occupying us, and then we hate our incapability of having other choices or of changing our destiny. Tell me, should I just let those Jewish settlers take over my house and live with that all my life? I can't. I simply can't." Abu Salem stopped to rethink what he said. He never thought of the conflict that way. The flashes of inspirations this mission had brought him amazed him probably more than they amazed his son.

Only distant sounds of early birds and barking dogs could be heard. Salem was unable to make up his mind, and he was also sure that making his father change his mind is impossible. For a moment, he thought of dragging him out of the house. Instead, he sat down near his father and watched him as he skillfully grouped the parts in a particular order.

"Are you sure, Dad?" asked Salem one last time.

"I am," interrupted his father, trying hard to control his shaky hands.

"Are you sure you know what you're doing?" repeated Salem, expecting the explosives to go off at any time.

"I have never been more certain in my life. Now just please leave me alone for a few minutes and keep watch outside," his father commanded.

"Ok, you be careful. The sun has started to rise," urged Salem.

"Funny that we fear the light. Funny that the dawn has become scary. You see, son, this is what I always tell you. They took my house—my history, my roots, and my land. And now, look at me, I am destroying it. This can't go on forever, and I can't rely on bastard politicians. Just go," insisted Abu Salem.

Salem did not like when talks with his father to turned to politics and politicians. Salem, though he sometimes admitted his father's insight, did not usually like his comments on political issues, let alone talking politics while piecing together a bomb. He lingered for a few seconds, unable to decide what to do next. Finally, Salem muttered something that sounded like "take care," and left.

After about fifteen minutes, his father squeezed himself out and signaled to Salem to move. He was carrying a mobile phone in his left hand and the brown bag, which obviously was empty, was on his back. Abu Salem stopped there for a little while to have a last look at the house and the area. The greenery extended as far as his eyes could see. In an instant, they both, dragging small branches of olive trees, made their way carefully but quickly back to where they came from.

"Dad, why didn't you leave the bag there?" inquired Salem sheepishly after ten minutes of trotting in silence at the first light of the day.

"I cannot leave it behind. If someone saw me carrying the bag on my way here and does not see it on my way back, he might become suspicious," replied Abu Salem in a manner that told he had given it a lot of thinking, which impressed Salem beyond imagination.

"Is it timed or remotely controlled?" asked Salem. "We need to be as far from our house as possible," he commented in an afterthought, expecting to hear an explosion any minute.

"Do not worry. We will make it just in time," said Abu Salem.

"How big do you think the explosion will be? Will we be able to hear it from here?" asked Salem, with concern clear in his voice.

Abu Salem, sensing the anxiety in his son's voice, decided finally to reveal what he actually did inside the house. "There will be no explosion...."

"What? No explosion! Why? Wasn't that a bomb you put? Answer me, Dad. You have put us and the whole family through this perilous quest of yours and we achieve nothing?"

"No, no. Not that. I put explosives. I just crammed the parts without connecting the wires."

"What?"

"You are right; it is mad to destroy the house. But I decided to keep the bomb there. I want them to fear. To live in fear. They have to feel that we are breathing down their necks. I want the Israelis to start asking questions," he said gesturing towards the Wall.

"Dad, they won't," commented Salem, trying hard to hide his relief, but amazed at his father's profundity of thinking and quick wit. "We could have been killed," he said.

"Listen, son, the worst thing about occupation is that they do not deal with intentions. That's why occupations are evil. Had they caught me with those explosives, I would have been shot dead—we would have been shot dead. They would not check on our intentions and if they did, they would not believe us. Occupation is evil. Yes, it steals and damages, but it also teaches people hate and, even worse, distrust. That's why leaving the bomb behind is a message: I can destroy the house but do not want to. Because I want people to start asking questions about the morality of their position towards us," he elaborated.

"You're my son and the closest to me," said Abu Salem. He stopped to take a breath, but Salem realized his father was rather seeking confirmation, and he quickly nodded eagerly in response, leaning his head a little to the right. "You're my son and the closest to me, and still you could not figure out what I really wanted to do. Perhaps you judged me. You thought I was crazy." This time Abu Salem did not take a breath to wait for confirmation. Salem shook his head anyway. "This doubt and mistrust will go on and on until people start asking questions, and when they do, answers will follow."

Salem saw his father smile all the way back home. Was it the way he worded his philosophy in life and resistance? Did he feel he had the upper hand over the occupation? Was it that he finally went back to his house even for a little while? Or was it that he took revenge in his own way?

◊

The next day, Israeli headlines were all about what Abu Salem did.

IDF FOILS A MAJOR TERROR ATTACK

JERUSALEM—Israeli Defense Forces dismantled on Saturday morning a remote-control bomb they found in a house in the settlement of Nili. No injuries reported.

The bomb was so huge it could have destroyed the whole house, army sources confirmed.

Neverland

by Tasnim Hamouda

DEALING WITH SERIOUS CASES HAD LONG BECOME PART OF HER life. And death had become a normality, an everyday experience. Her hard work and dearest wishes had not helped. Getting attached to cases had not helped either. She decided to give up on names, but not on hope and certainly not on hard work. Names create memories. Names form attachment. And she definitely did not want that. Not again. But she simply couldn't detach herself from those little passing clouds. She could not just leave them and move to another section of the hospital that treats less serious cases, cases with hope of survival. All she knew is that she was now attached to death in mysterious ways. She believed she was destined to deal with death, to look it in the eye every day, and to conquer it every day. And every time she failed—and failed miserably.

Sooner than anyone expects, faster than it takes to memorize their names, death would perch on the ward, extend its wings right and left, and claim them all. A week, two weeks—a month maximum—and new faces would replace the previous ones. Similar faces with different names all would share the same fate.

There were seven in each ward, all of whom she called "little boy" or "little girl." At nine o'clock every night, she would check them in turn. "It's your injection time, little boy," she said, asking him to stretch out his arm, which she barely touched. She had learned how to distract herself when giving the children their shots. Sometimes she gazed at the ceiling or looked at the door that stood far from the six nearby beds she still needed to examine.

Every time she reached the last bed, there was the same little boy who would welcome her with a smile, maybe the mightiest thing he could do. "It's your injection time, little boy." He hid a book under his pillow, got his injection, and was left to sleep afterward. She would linger there awkwardly, trying to catch a glimpse of the book. He pushed the book further under the pillow. For two months, she had done the same thing. It pained her that this little one had to see all those faces come and go. It pained her that he had to change friends three or four times—not that he had a choice. Once she was done with him, she would rush out of the ward. Her mission for the night had been accomplished.

The next morning, she appeared again on an emergency call as another "little one" was moved to her ward. There are eight now, she thought. At nine, again, it was injection time. Bruised arms were stretched. Eyes, half closed, fixed on the ceiling. And one last bed to check.

By the time she reached him, the book this time lying open on his chest, his hairless head leaning on the edge of the pillow, he didn't smile. She sat, almost motionlessly, next to him and picked up the book. It was *Peter Pan*, the tale of the boy who never grows up and spends his never-ending childhood on the small island of Neverland where forgotten boys live.

She put the book back in his little, cold hands, wishing he was able to finish the story. "Sleep tight, little b...little Peter Pan," she murmured.

Lost at Once

by Elham Hilles

HE NEVER FELT HOW MY SOUL LEAPED AND HOW MY HEARTBEAT turned into the loudest discordant drums whenever I heard his voice. Contradicting thoughts filled my head whenever his image appeared. I was captured by every detail of his manliness—so witty, so sharp, such a charming man who philosophizes everything he says or hears. "Dear me, what a happy girl I am!" I always exclaimed after hanging up my cell phone with him. "This is the exact type of guy I've always dreamed of." I couldn't ask for more, though I had never even thought of asking him where he lived. Why should I bother myself to ask? I always supposed—or to tell the truth, I was programmed to expect—that everybody I met in my city was originally Gazan.

"Oh, girl...." I got to know that these were the words he often used whenever he shocked me with a real detail about himself. "Eman, if you just knew where exactly I live, you wouldn't be stupidly in love with everything related to me." Hosam kept upsetting my soul and driving me crazy by repeating these annoying words. It was something I couldn't figure out in that stage of my immaturity—or, maybe, my innocence.

"But why the hell should I care where you live? Aren't you from Gaza? That is quite enough to keep my hope alive."

I was too naïve to go deeper into any other details.

"Look, Hosam," I said. "All I want is a mind and a tongue—a powerful mind to appreciate me, and an expressive, eloquent tongue, to say it."

"Well, I doubt it. What should a woman do with a man's mind and tongue if they got married? Did you forget that I'm a lawyer? It's the core of my profession to talk and manipulate things," he said, teasingly.

"Ok, let's not think about it now...I don't care where you live, and that's it." I added, looking at my watch, which said 4:25 in the afternoon, "Oh my God! I have to leave the library right away." I hung up my cell phone and rushed outside.

"Al-Mina—to the seaport, please," I told the taxi driver in a hurry.

He drove his car and stopped after a few meters for some university students who were heading to Al-Nasr Street.

"Don't be angry. I'll drive as fast as I can to drop them off, and then I'll take you wherever you wish," the old, big-mouthed driver said.

"But Al-Nasr is not my way. Why did you take me in the first place?" I asked furiously. And then, to stop the dispute, I added despairingly, "It's okay. Just drive."

Praying that my father would not be home when I got back, I just kept looking outside the window, thinking of excuses for my delay. I thought of how careless I was in doing the same thing every day, spending two or three hours in the central library, looking for Ghada Al-Samman, Badr Shakir Al-Sayyab, Nazik Al-Mala'ika, and other Arab poets and writers whom I recently became extremely fond of. I never expected to reach that point: not attending my lectures and sitting alone in the back when I attend, alienating myself between the pages of Gibran Khalil Gibran, Khalil Mutran, Michael Naimeh, and all those sorts of writers. That was the biggest sin, yet the most precious favor, any man has ever done for me. Hosam's talks about these writers always made me envious and in quest of more and more reading. I fell in love with everything he liked.

I woke up from my deep thoughts quite abruptly to find myself in a very remote area which I'd never been to.

"What is this place? You said you were going to take the girls to Al-Nasr Street, right? Where am I?" I questioned in a panic. "I'm sorry, but I was obliged to go further. The car is running out of fuel, and the petroleum station is here. I'll be back soon." Getting out of the car, he added, "Do you want me to turn on some music? I have several songs for Mustafa Kamel; he is very good, you know. Do you want me to change the song? Tell me, what is your favorite song of his?"

I kept silent and didn't utter a word, lest he should go further. Anxious and scared of staying in the car, I looked outside to make sure that the man was busy. I ran out of the taxi, and then went on walking in streets I had never passed before.

"O my goodness! It's nearly five o'clock. How can I find another taxi in these narrow streets?" I nearly cried. I wondered how I got lost in this little space.

I went on walking, heading toward the west. A group of school boys fighting attracted my attention. I could not help stopping and asking them.

"What is the name of this place, little boys?"

"*Mo'askaaar Al-Shati. Mesh 'arfaah?*"–Al-Shati Refugee Camp. Don't you know it?—shouted the chubby boy.

"Okay, why are you angry?"

"*Hada al-kalb,*" pointing at another boy, "*sarag nossi!*"–Because this dog stole my half shekel—he yelled.

"It's mine. *Ummy*—my mother—gave it to me," replied the smaller one.

Their accent brought a smile on my face. For me it is "Mama," always "Mama."

"Here's a shekel instead," I said to the angry boy. "Just don't fight, okay?" I added, trying to imitate his tone. I failed.

"Hehehe! Shayef jazat elli bysrig? Hay shekel badal al-nos!"—
See how God punishes those who steal? I have a shekel now
instead of a half one!—the boy teased his friend, laughing out
loud, not believing that he got a whole shekel.

I had always heard about the dire circumstances of the
Palestinian refugees, but I had never taken the time to visit any
of the places they lived. Al-Shati camp is not so far from Al-
Mina area, but I was always made to believe that these places
were way too remote.

All these thoughts came into my mind while I was going
deeper into the unpaved, narrow roads of the camp; no taxis
were there to pick me up and take me back home. Lines of
squalid semi-houses were lying along the two sides of the roads.
The biggest of them was about one hundred square meters. They
looked like boxes—not shaped beautifully, nor painted, and
nearly crumbling. Most of their windows were broken, allowing
Gaza's summer heat to radiate inside, and not preventing the
winter's cold and rainwater from bothering their inhabitants. A
stream of water was like an anaconda halving the alley into two
parts. The fetid smell was overwhelming.

Soon I saw that wretched view of sewage, which was almost
going inside one of the houses. The roofs of most of them were
made of meager pieces of metal or wood, which seemed to allow
water to go through. If two juxtaposed houses were separated
by a mere meter and a half, then the two of them were blessed
enough not to hear their neighbors snoring at night. I wondered
what degree of privacy any of them could have. Then I figured
that privacy was the last concern for people who were so deprived of their basic needs as human beings. It seemed to me
that privacy was a luxury those people did not afford. If it had
not been for those rugs dangling behind or in front of the doors,
I would have seen inside the houses just by walking past them.

Walking further, I came across two old men sitting under a
huge old ziziphus tree, which stood there alone between a pair
of houses. They were sitting on small wooden chairs. I wanted

to ask them for directions, but then decided to listen to their conversation. I walked as slowly as I could.

"I swear that a cluster of grapes in our village, Yibna, was a hundred times better than ten kilos of these grapes, *ya zalama*—man," said one of the men while eating some black grapes.

"*Wallah*—I swear to God—you're right. May God's mercy engulf us and take us back there before we die," the other man said.

"Look at your white beard, old man!"

"Allah is all powerful. I'm going to see my village *insha'Allah*—God willing. And even if I die before then, I'll ask Allah to give me some of its grapes in heaven."

Their voices faded away as I proceeded further toward the western part of Gaza.

I was shocked when I soon reached the coastal road, where my family lived. I realized how close to the refugee camp my neighborhood was. For the first time, I did not feel any safer seeing the familiar faces and familiar buildings and shops. I realized then the difference between them—and us. I stopped to contemplate the houses and buildings that I was used to passing every day, without giving them a mere glance. Two-story houses. Three-story houses. Four-story houses. All with marble walls. All with glass covering huge parts of their facades. The streets in our neighborhood were wide, so wide. The shadow of seven or eight fifteen-story buildings as the sun leaned further toward the sea must have extended to engulf those abysmal rooms in the camp.

The magnificence of these constructions was not the thing that engrossed me, but it was the radical difference that existed. The thorough division between that clean, well-structured place, which is not even a hundred meters away from the camp, is the tragedy that distressed me. Dozens of well-dressed men and women were going into Aldeira Hotel, where four or five thousand dollars would be paid just to hold a wedding party with an open buffet. It was more than enough to build a new room for a refugee family. How on earth was this chasm created when only a couple of decades ago we lived almost equally?

The glorious scene of twilight indicated that the maghrib prayer would be called within a few minutes. I breathed a sigh of relief upon seeing that my father's car was not parked outside the house. I rushed inside and went upstairs on my tiptoes, looking around and becoming nervous at any sound I heard.

"Why should I scold you every day for the same thing? I swear that your feelings are so cold, that's if you have any sort of feelings! When are you going to grow up and be responsible?" Mama burst into her usual lectures. "Your father is not home now, but imagine, just imagine, that he saw you come home at five-thirty! This is the last time for you to come home late. Next time, I'll tell him. And you know what's going to happen..." she continued with the same high-pitched voice.

My dear mother has always scolded me in that same way, threatening me every time that she would tell my father. She never did; instead, she would forget the whole thing in an hour, just because I gave her a hand in washing the dishes or some other household task. I always asked her if all the mothers of the world have the same motherhood gene that makes them forget all the bad things their children did. She would only answer me by saying, "You won't know that unless you have a baby."

I locked myself inside the room and started flashing back to all the scenes I observed. I needed to call Hosam at that very moment.

"Could he be...?" Not daring to keep on imagining that idea, I dialed his number in order to get some relief. And while his cell phone was ringing, I told myself that if he really was from the camp, then I would definitely excuse him for not telling me where he lived.

"Did your father beat the hell out of you?" said Hosam, mockingly.

"Well, you know that I would not be here to talk to you if he had done that. Mama, as usual, saved my life," I replied.

"'Mama'? You're a university student and you still say 'mama,'" he mocked again. "It's *ummy*," he added.

It all added up now. This time his voice sounded like those of the people I had just met. "Oh my God, how didn't I notice that before? Some of your words are like the accent of those who live in the camps."

"What are you trying to say?" he asked. "Have you reached any new detail about my residence during your daily Googling for my identity?"

"You're a refugee. And that's why you kept it a secret from me. Hosam, I don't think it's a shameful thing for you to be a refugee. Just tell me; I'm ready to accept any reality."

"Oh, really? Ready? Are you trying to tell me that accepting me as I am is a concession from your majesty? You, Gazan!"

"I've already accepted everything about you. I only want you to love who you are. Don't conceal yourself."

He breathed a deep sigh and started talking. "Yes, my lady. I am a refugee. I swear by every part and every tree of this camp. I swear by the sky and the air of this camp, that I'm a refugee. I live in Al-Nusseirat refugee camp...."

"Yeah, I studied that in geography. Is that near Khan Yunus and Deir Al-Balah?" I asked innocently, interrupting his touching speech.

"Are you serious? You seem to have never visited this camp. It's past Al-Zahra City. Khan Yunus is far from here."

He seemed totally aware of all the places of Gaza Strip, while I felt very reluctant of telling him that, only an hour ago, I was lost in Al-Shati Camp, which is only a few hundred meters away from where I live. So, it was in no way expected from a girl who had never left her immediate surroundings to recognize where exactly Al-Nusseirat camp is.

I tried to appear as calm as I could. Still, imagining the area was torture in itself. A stream of endless questions came to my mind. Would I be doomed to live in a similar place when we get married? Is Al-Nusseirat camp similar to the one I went by?

I hastened towards my computer and wrote the name of that camp on Google Earth. Several images of the place demonstrated that it was a lot better than Al-Shati Camp. "Such a fool I am.... He has never mentioned anything about marriage. Why should I believe that he's going to be my husband?" I thought.

I dared to ask my mother if my father would accept a refugee suitor to be my husband. She whispered, "Are you dreaming? He'll want to know the guy's original town. He should be a Gazan."

Thrown into despair, I headed to my room, cursing the unfair standards we had to live by.

◊

And now, here I am. Four years later, I am another refugee's wife. And I still reminisce about Hosam. He never ceased to be an essential part of my growing up, of my initiation from dreams to reality.

A month ago, I checked the e-mail that I had used years ago to communicate with Hosam. An unread message from him was waiting for me. It was sent two months earlier. I burst into tears upon seeing the name.

Dear Eman,

After four years of your marriage, as well as my losing you to another man, whom I hate from the depths of my heart, though I don't even know anything about him, I could never forget you. Never could I forgive myself for losing you. I'd never expected that four years were enough for a stubborn man to establish himself.

Eman, when I decided to end our relationship, I claimed I was trying to protect you from me and from your Dad and from a harsh world. I guess I was lying. I was too ashamed and cowardly to approach him to ask for your hand. I guess, for the little I have, I felt too arrogant to feel rejected. Only now do I realize that you have been an adventure worthy of anything.

Such a foolish man I was, dear Eman, for not having the courage to knock on your father's door in order to tell him "I want your daughter." I thought that a Gazan driving a fifty-thousand dollar Mercedes would just kick me out of his house if I dared to ask him for his daughter's hand. I couldn't endure imagining that idea then. Such a fool I am. Such a fool I am.

Hosam

It's My Loaf of Bread

by Tasnim Hamouda

"THIS PRECIOUS LOAF OF BREAD I'M HOLDING IN MY HANDS, fellows, has an epic story behind it," declared the little boy standing on a small wooden chair. "I promised I would get it, and here it is," he boasted.

His friends, who had gathered from every corner, route, and slum of the city, listened carefully as their little companion spoke proudly of how he managed to get their promised loaf back after those long days they spent watching the bread on sellers' carts roaming the city, leaving them with nothing but an irresistible aroma. It was the same aroma their parents and grandparents smelled for years but never gained.

The little one continued, "He was a big, old man. The biggest man I have ever seen. He wore a strangely striped cloth of black and white on his head...."

"A kufiya. That's how I heard them call it," a friend interrupted.

"Hush! They don't have to know this," whispered the little boy as he drew his head closer to his companion's shoulder. His small audience was so enchanted by the loaf of bread that they didn't notice this stealthy interaction. He adjusted his kippah on his head and went on, "I watched him day and night. He spread the bread on a small wooden pushcart as if it was ordinary bread. Oh, my friends, my heart bled seeing this happen to our bread. But I was patient and stood still until that one sparkling moment came. I walked slowly towards him, captured this loaf of bread, and ran away, with the old man's cries chasing me."

"Did he chase you?" a voice came from the crowd.

"At first he did not move. Maybe he didn't see it coming."

Maybe the story would not have been this interesting to his audience had he told them the rest of it: how he wasn't the fast runner he thought he was and how he had almost been caught and how he begged the policeman for mercy. He did not tell them of the police who insisted, despite the old man's pleas, to compromise. The police gave the boy only a crust and returned the rest to the old man. Still, his friends were even more captivated when he drew the bread near his beaming mouth and gulped a big part of it.

"What happened next?" someone asked.

"I felt sorry for the old, breathless man. He must have hated the fact that a youngster like myself had defeated him," chuckled the boy, his voice choked by ultimate triumph rather than stolen bread. "You felt sorry? Are you saying you want to give it back to him?" a curious question arose.

"No, I snuck back and took the rest," said the little one as he gulped the last bit of the old man's bread.

Once Upon a Dawn

by Shahd Awadallah

It was one of the wintriest and blackest nights, the darkness gloomily wrapping Gaza's narrow streets and sleeping people in its extended black blanket.

That night, all sounds were hushed, almost reverent in sympathy with Gaza's second, sad anniversary of the Israeli war, which left a deep wound inside each heart and soul. I was asleep, or to be more accurate, I was feigning sleep, until the warm drop of a salty tear burned its way smoothly and slowly upon the upper part of my cheek, ending its journey in a trembling fall on the edge of my ear. It silently sank on my white, cold pillow. That lonely drop was followed by a flood of uncountable tears that rushed fast to express their utter grief. They stifled me. I got up in a desperate try to escape that wet, salty pillow, heartily confident that I will never be able to escape those melancholic recollections which occupied most of my memory and my whole life.

A shrunken, white piece of paper and a black pen were the first things I beheld after I got up. They were lying on my honey-colored, crowded desk, located on the left side of my bed. I sat at my desk, holding the sheet of paper in my right hand

144 Gaza Writes Back

and the pen in the left. "This is a good chance to challenge your sorrow; if you fail, as usual, you will have to live with more pain and more sleepless nights." These were the words my bleary mind and aching heart would pronounce ever since I had lost my much-praised abilities to express myself through words, the means that used to be my advocate whenever I got the chance to hold a pen and write. This night, I decided to follow the calls of my soul. They were calm and calling for me peacefully to write a letter to the innocent kid I lost that night.

The orange rays of the street lights added great solemnity to the holiness of the night's darkness, and melted with it to create a new fiery color that surprisingly took my breath away, slipping smoothly through the western window I had opened earlier and reflecting upon the desk where I was sitting motionless. The rays illumined my soul and inflamed my desire to pick up a new paper to write a complete letter to admit my fatal fault and announce my truthful repentance in order to get rid of this torturing regret. At last, I put my pen to the paper and started to ruin its purity with some connected black lines that formed the characters of my letter.

My dear son,

I really want you to read each and every single word I write here, because I am no longer able to keep the story in my heart. I promise this time I will try to complete the letter. I promise I will not tear it up. For I need you to understand what happened. I need to explain to you because you were asleep when you died, when you were slain. Every single memory tortures me and reminds me of that cursed night.

It was a cold night; can you remember it?

Seconds passed and I got no answer. I submissively continued.

I am sure you can. It was really cold. You were lying asleep beside me. Your warm breaths were blowing near my face and neck. Your heartbeats were harmonically delicate. I was used to them. They were the soft recital which I could never sleep without first feeling, while contemplating your face's perfectly created features. I have lost that innocence when I lost you that night. You doubt it, right? It is the absolute truth, my child.

Again, I waited, but I got nothing except the remains of my stifled words, the words I have never said. I resumed.

We—you and me, and my mother, father, brothers, and sisters—were all asleep in the dining room of our house. We thought it would be the safest room. Alas! It wasn't. Nights before, Dad suggested that we all should leave our rooms and sleep together in the dining room, because our rooms had windows that might break as a result of the bombings which dominated Gaza's nights and days. We all moved to the dining room.

The western winds continued blowing softly through the window behind me. It had been one of my habits to sleep with the window open to rid myself of the smell of death and the grave-like silence that kept reminding me of my loneliness. A tremor shook my body while I was recalling memories and waiting insanely for my son's answers. The western wind turned me into a piece of marble in the darkness of the freezing winter. It felt cleansing for a little while, spreading its wings of purity. However, its attempts were all in vain. I remained wounded.

It started thundering and raining. Little crystal drops of rain sneaked with the wind into the room and lightly hit me, then trickled down my naked neck. I trembled again. A tiny smile slipped away from my lips when the smell of the muddy earth started to fill the quivering air.

It is raining. A few days before that night, it was silent except for the noisy rain. How cute your picture was when I painted you sitting underneath the rain. Actually, you weren't out under the rain on that day. Hairless and cold, you were seated, with your strawberry-colored lips and childish looks, like those of a kitten begging for love, exhaling your breaths on the freezing window, creating your own world of steam only to scribble it with your tiny fingers. You laughed your heart out as you painted a new world of steam, and spoiled it again and again. At that very moment, I was enjoying the same sound of rain and the same smell of earth. I was drawing you with the tiniest detail of the chuckles you gave whenever a few raindrops softly fell on your bald head.

You didn't like it when I teased you with an instigating smile, calling you "bald kid." Sometimes, you would cry, tearing my heart apart, and other times you would laugh charmingly. I couldn't understand it, but I liked it when I called you "bald kid." Are you crying or laughing now, my son? Does my calling you bald now that you're a year older make you happy or angry? I wish I knew.

In that picture, some raindrops were on your head, others on your eyelashes, trembling slightly. With shiny, dark eyes, you were sitting on the wet grass laughing. You liked that picture as much as I liked the rain; I lost it the same night I lost your glittering eyes and delightful smile....

Two teardrops were imprisoned at the edge of my eyes. They finally prevailed.

That night at 4:50 a.m., my alarm clock woke me up to the peaceful sound of a folk song in which the singer asks his mother not to be sad after his martyrdom, for he will be in paradise. I always liked it, but not after what happened later that night. It now revolts me. I turned the alarm off in order not to annoy you and the other sleepers in the room. I got up, seeking a prayer before the dawn prayer time. You were fast asleep. Others in the room were sound asleep after a long battle with sleeplessness due to the buzzing of dozens of warplanes that had been hovering over Gaza for two weeks. Darkness dominated the scene. I turned my flashlight on to avoid stepping on my brothers, who were sleeping on the floor. Peacefully, I passed, got ready for praying, and entered my room with a sense of longing invading my heart, reminding me of the long nights and days spent there telling stories about the melted past and the coming bright future. The future seemed to decay that night. Hope seemed to be thinning. Only you gave me hope; only your future gave mine a purpose.

I started to pray and implored God to save my family and our home. A moment before I ended my prayer, a massive explosion shook the building, drilling my ears and throwing me meters away from my prayer rug. The explosion was paired with a terrifying sound of glass crashing in and out of the house. Terribly frightened, I ran toward the dining room where you and the family were. They all got up holding their flashlights, running instinctively with horror, making sure everyone was okay. They had only small cuts. Seconds passed and everything was calm again, and the holiness of darkness and quietness controlled the scene. You remained asleep. I have to admit, I smiled when I saw you asleep. You did not care. My mother was still worried and asked my brother to go with her to make sure that our uncle's family, who has an apartment beside ours, was okay. My uncle opened his door at the same time that Mom and my brother opened ours. He said, "Don't worry. We are all okay, but what was that? What did they target..." Before the end of his words, a greater explosion took place on the stairs between the two apartments.

The whole building quaked. White dust rose and covered the place. Rubble violently rushed into the apartment. The doors came off their hinges. Everyone was shaken. And you were still asleep. For a few moments, I forgot you. Mom started to shout, "Say the shahada and go downstairs! Get out of the building! These missiles are targeting us!"

I put my pen down in a depressed attempt to stop the flood of the painful memories that started rushing into my exhausted mind. I couldn't. My son should know each detail in order to forgive me. I went on.

Mom's words stayed in my ears: "Say the shahada and go downstairs." However, I didn't leave right away. I went to the dining room to fetch you, yet I passed through my room on my way to the dining room to have a last look and paint the last picture of it in my mind. I saw my now disorganized text books which had been waiting for the end of that hideous war and begging me to hold them again as I used to do since I joined college after your father's martyrdom two years ago. I saw my crowded bookshelves, my closet, my prayer rug, and even my red glasses. All were scattered here and there. My mother's voice reverted strongly: "Say the shahada and go downstairs." I wasn't aware of anything; I left my room headed toward the dining room to get you when I saw my weeping young cousins entering our apartment instead of going downstairs. It was extremely dark, and they were crying loudly. I asked one of them, "What are you doing here? Why don't you go down?" With a trembling voice he answered, "There's no flashlight. We can't see." I was really worried that one of them might enter another room and be forgotten in the darkness. "Come kids, follow me," I said and took them quickly.

"I can't walk; the stones are hurting my foot. I want my shoes," one of them said. "Please, bring me my shoes."

"No time, dear. We will bring them later." I was wholly sure that we would never be able to bring them ever again.

Seconds after our exit, the third missile hit the third floor, where we were.

"I was there, Mom. You left me there, Mom. I was alone with nothing but my tears and mournful cries, Mom." My son's voice penetrated my ears. I dropped my pen as chills ran through my body. Shockingly, he was sitting in front of me with his white robe, bald head, and shiny eyes, gazing at my teary, black eyes, smiling and saying, "I'm home alone, Mom." I couldn't handle the shock and remained silent for a little while, staring back at the blurry image of my son.

Nature's anger increased; the thunder started to become louder, the western winds became stronger, a lightning bolt illuminated the room, and my kid looked like a white, bright ghost with inflamed eyes. I could utter no word while my son's voice became quieter, repeating the same sentence: "I was alone, Mom. I was alone, Mom. I was alone..." and then disappeared.

I made no movement and said nothing until a breeze blew over my body and gave life to my consciousness again. Hesitantly, I held my pen again. Determined to continue till the end, I wrote.

We stayed for nearly three minutes at our neighbor's house, waiting for the last missile which put an end to the story of our home, when the holy sound of the dawn prayer calls interrupted the hardest moments of waiting: "Allah is the Greatest; Allah is the Grea...." The massive explosion of the F-16 missile vaporized the sound of the prayer calls and deafened us. My body sagged in agony, and I whispered, "It's gone." Seconds later, I left our neighbor's house and saw ours burning like a volcano. Nothing but fire. I thought of nothing. I said nothing and did nothing except gaze at the burning memories of my life with my heart vanishing, when suddenly your picture flashed in my mind. I started running unconsciously towards the burning building, calling your name and bursting into tears, when my father grasped my arm, firmly preventing me from going there. He was sure that you had died. Nothing could survive that blaze, let alone thirty pounds of tender flesh. They shouted for the fire engine and the ambulance to help. The scene was too excruciating to bear. I fainted.

That night, I lost you. I remembered you again when I woke up in the hospital. I remembered that I forgot you alone there. I realized that I will be all alone after your and your father's martyrdom. You are alone, and I am alone. You will stay alone. I will stay alone. You died alone, and I will die alone. That night, I missed your warm breaths, harmonic heartbeats, and charming smile. That night, I lost my son.

My pen calmly fell down, my tears abundantly welled up, my head heavily struck the table, and mournfully, I wept. My tongue couldn't stop repeating the word "alone," infesting the silence of that night. I heard nothing but my mother's whisper. "I pity her," she said. "She is still lamenting. She keeps on writing every night but those who die never come back."

She kept on whispering, and I kept on lamenting, "Together we lived, and alone you died."

The Old Man and the Stone

by Refaat Alareer

"...And I want you to bury it with me. That's my will. I have had it for ages. I never let it out of my sight or my pocket. Do you remember your Uncle Sadek who, God bless his soul, passed away when you were five years old?" said Abu Yusef, only stopping for a second to catch a breath. He genuinely did not want to give his son, Yusef, the time to answer his question. Life had taught him two fragments of wisdom: kids will never ever understand his passion for things, and if they do, their opinions usually indicate shallowness of thinking.

"Only vaguely," Yusef interrupted him anyway.

"He brought it from Jerusalem. He thought I was crazy. He thought I was being silly because I kept asking him to bring me a stone or a handful of sand when he goes to Jerusalem. I am never silly or kidding when it comes to Jerusalem." Seeing that his son was distracted, Abu Yusef elbowed him.

"Dad, how can you do it?" interrupted Yusef, again.

"Do what?" inquired his father.

"Tell a story with such passion," said the son, half kidding and half serious.

"So when I say bury it with me, I mean bury it with me. Make sure to slip it in my hand. I am sure my grip will hold onto it. But if it does not, you can tie it in my fist," said the old man, ignoring his son, not detecting or perhaps not wanting to detect his sarcasm.

"Father, you are still young. Why would you want to die this young?" replied Yusef.

"And make sure everyone knows about it. It is no secret. And it should not be kept a secret. I know you would be ashamed to tell others about a stone, thinking I am insane. But even your uncle, the most stubborn man that ever walked on earth, was finally convinced and brought it. Maybe he wanted to make me stop nagging or maybe he did not want me to leave home and take a long, arduous journey to Jerusalem to get a stone. I do not care about the reason; he got a stone for me. From Jerusalem. A stone from Jerusalem. Unlike those people you see every day, I am far better than them all. I own part of Jerusalem," replied the old man, his voice rising every time he said "Jerusalem."

"Dad, if everyone who loves Jerusalem brings a stone, a rock, or a handful of sand, we will no longer have Jerusalem. We will run out of Jerusalem. A picture would have saved you all the trouble and the embarrassment caused by that thing...."

"It is not a thing," interrupted the man, almost mechanically.

"What's that?" inquired Yusef.

"The stone. It is not a thing. It is a stone. From Jerusalem..." said Abu Yusef, a touch of impatience underlying his explanation.

"Okay, okay, Dad. Okay, it is a stone. The stone!" bellowed Yusef.

"A picture is not going to be like a stone that has been subjected to the rain and the heat and the cold and the dirt and the smell of Jerusalem. This stone is Jerusalem. It is," was the man's reply, adding extra emphasis this time on every word and taking a short breath between words.

"How so?" asked Yusef, who had heard the very same answer hundreds of times.

"I have never forgotten Jerusalem for even one day since I got this stone thirteen years and two months ago. When your uncle gave it to me, I was...."

"Dad, do you still want to go visit my sister next week?" interrupted Yusef intentionally, in an attempt to change the topic.

"Yes," snapped the old man. "I would swear that sometimes this stone wakes me at dawn to pray *al-fajr*."

"Of course it does. If you sleep with the stone in your pocket and you turn to sleep on the side where you put the stone, it will wake you up," Yusef retorted with heavy sarcasm.

"You do not understand. You really do not. It is not like that. I mean...."

In another attempt to cut short an elongated explanation of the old man, Yusef asked, "Can I hold it, father?"

"Uhh..." came his father's reply. Surprised by his son's sudden interest in the stone, he found it a bit hard to let go of it.

"Dad? Can I hold it?"

"Okay, but be careful," replied his father, hesitatingly.

"Okay," said Yusef, hurriedly extending his hand to hold the stone.

"Careful, I say!" yelled the old man.

"Dad, this is too much. This has really become embarrassing and annoying. 'The stone! The stone! The stone....'"

"Shut up!" his father shouted, red-faced, hastily grabbing the stone back.

"I'll tell you something. Your nephew Ahmed told me long ago that Uncle Sadek lied to you," Yusef replied, this time his voice getting louder than his father's.

"What do you mean 'lied to you'?" asked the old man with a commanding voice, hoping his son was only saying that to tease him.

"He told his sons before he passed away to tell you the truth about the stone. It is simply not from Jerusalem. It is a *false* stone," came Yusef's reply.

"What do you mean? What do you m-m-mean not from Jerusalem? If he told them, why did they not come to tell me?" asked his father.

"They know you very well, Dad. They were afraid that the truth might kill you! He said he felt too stupid to bend down and pick up a stone. So he got you one he found in front of his house. A false stone," explained Yusef, regretting he ever broke the news he had struggled to keep secret for years.

"Stop lying to me! And stop saying 'false'. It is *not* false! God damn it!" yelled his father bitterly. He never used that word before.

"I am not lying!" Yusef retorted.

"May he rot in hell! Too stupid to bend down in...in Jerusalem?" growled Abu Yusef, his anger rising like never before. He had never insulted his brother.

"Take it easy, Dad," muttered his son, in a faint voice. He knew very well what his father does in his fits of rage.

"Take it easy?" echoed Abu Yusef, "Now he is rotting in h... he is...give me that stone...give it to me...ahh ahhh...." Putting his left hand on his chest, trying to breathe, Abu Yusef fell, his eyes wide-open staring up, his right hand clutching at the stone.

"Dad! Daaad! Dad, stay with me! Stay with me! Daaaaad!"

Scars

by Aya Rabah

I WANTED TO BE ALONE AND ESCAPE EVERYTHING. I ALWAYS dreamed to be like a blooming flower, covered with that magical meaning of warmth and life.

I missed my son, Salam, meaning peace, and my daughter, Hayat, meaning life. I could not figure out why I chose these names for both of them, but maybe it was my way to defy the atmosphere of the world they came into.

◊

I used to hear my mother's shouts coming out of the kitchen, my brothers' joyful yells reaching everywhere.

Then everything was gone—my mother, my brothers. The tormenting smells filled our home. The sun's rays, forming transparent wings like those of a guardian angel, held the house. Then I could see nothing but dark peace. Yes, even peace can be dark.

I still vividly see my mother's pale face like a full moon. "You are so selfish," my mother always told me. I did not know what made her see me like that.

After the accident, I thought of a good explanation: I am the only survivor of my family; I wanted life to be only for me. I should spend the rest of my life trying to get rid of this trait. Being selfish was something painted upon my forehead by my mother's words.

My brothers' yells still sound like thunder everywhere I go. Their dismembered bodies are still emerging in my dreams like blinding flashes. They were buried under concrete rubble of our old house along with their fears and despair—or hope, maybe, which will no longer be fulfilled in this cruel world. No one can know what their last thoughts were. Now that they are gone, all I can do is to imagine if they were bright or dark.

That wheat field behind our house is still shining with old, tired memories. The only thing that has changed is my way of seeing it.

"It is the land of battles," I pointed to Hayat, the first time I went there again. For ages, I could not face the terrible fact of being the only survivor of a horrible massacre.

It was one o'clock in the morning. The air's loose strings were circling me like ghosts. I asked my mother, "If something bad happens to us, what should I do?"

"Escape, sweetheart."

"Where?"

"To God, to God's heavens, darling."

I smiled.

My mother's words seemed to be taken from a sacred book. She was the one who escaped, not me. She escaped with the winter's wind, like the falling leaves of autumn.

My mother was like a holy figure standing in the shadow of God's throne whenever she picked lavender from our backyard. And because I was afraid of them—of the invader of our land—she always reminded me, "The more morals die inside a human being, the more crimes he will be able to commit." I thought I forgot that. Yet, strangely, when things happen, especially bad things, I immediately recall past advice, wisdom, or warning.

When I was awakened at the hospital, I did not need any clues to feel the change that happened to me. I turned to the nurse and asked her, "Are you real?"

"Do not worry. You are at the hospital. You are not severely injured. It's okay."

In hospitals, most of the time we are told things we already know or are afraid of. I could see her white uniform, and I still remember when they put me in the ambulance without covering my face as they did with my family. I wished I could tell her I knew. But I kept silent. All I wanted was a much simpler answer—an answer telling me it was just a dream and everything will be okay, an answer that could sound like a perfect lie rather than reporting reality in such a harsh way.

I tried to smile at the nurse, but I couldn't. I felt as if there was a mask on my face.

"My face?" I asked.

"It is just a superficial wound; do not worry. It will heal in no time," she reassured me.

I did not want her to explain, because it all seemed trivial at the time. Nothing mattered: not my face, nor my future—not even the war I survived, which taught me the meaning of loss. In fact, I did not want my wound to heal. I was satisfied with such tangible shame that could at least make me always remember those who lost their lives so others could survive. I could not run away from my shame this time. I do not want to. People outside must be recovering now from the war, I thought. I felt as if Gaza had turned into a vast hospital where everyone was suffering.

Even now, I am still grateful to the air which carried my soul over woods, mountains, and clouds, that air which helped my hand move tenderly up and touch the bloody scar boldly. It was heaped up with blisters. I thought, "Things may sound peaceful if we do not think about them, but once we do, they evoke harsh memories in our minds."

I became a girl with a scar.

◊

The scene behind my son, Salam, looked perfectly like an old painting, but his cynical smile disrupted the symmetry. It was a remarkable thing about him that he never smiled when I stood in front of him. I gently touched the burning scar across my left cheek. He was looking at me as if in a kind of silent attack. Behind him extended vast fields of green corn, emerging like the grandeur of paradise. I wanted to make him smile. I wanted to link him as a child to the perfection of the scene. He would not listen, his sympathetic eyes fixed on the tragic story starkly portrayed upon my cheek.

"Forgive me, but I need you to smile for the camera, son."

"I cannot. I do not like cameras. I do not like pictures."

I left his room as I did not want to bother him, my only son.

◊

"Do you think history repeats itself?" my history teacher once asked me unexpectedly.

It was hot and I felt sweaty. I could hardly breathe. This question hit me hard. I was broken. I stood hiding my cheek—I used to do that whenever I was the center of attention—then cried. I cried until I could no longer feel the awful heat; it was like being in a bubble, hearing nothing but my deeply buried memories. Everybody in the class, including me, was stunned by my reaction. After a while, the teacher told me to sit again. I finally spoke, "People all turn into dust at the end, teacher. I think history does not repeat itself, yet when we go back in time, by thinking, our memories dominate our present and future." I knew how much hypocrisy my answer implied, for what I thought about was my mother's scar on her right shoulder.

My history teacher did not accept my answer; she believed in a highly organized world, though it meant repeated pain that so many would encounter again and again. I have to confess that, as time passed, I came to agree with my teacher that history is always repeating itself, not necessarily in the same form, but it brings the same deformity to us.

◊

While taking the lives of my family one by one, death stood over my body and spared me. I did not want to pass. It was August and I wanted my body to melt over the breathing sand. Why did he let me go? Why did death not consider me a suspect and put me in jail? Why did it take Hayat and let me live instead?

It was not a time of war when she died, but it was not a time of peace either. A shell killed my family, and a fatal disease took my Hayat. Illness, like a bullet, invaded her body. There were no goodbyes, only wonders of why everything had to happen that way.

Every time I face trouble, I blame my scar. It's like a curse. It made me marry a man with one hand and later tortured my children every time they looked at me. Nobody likes the de-formed, except their Creator.

My daughter's disease was a declaration of war. Even before she was sick, she saw death everywhere.

"A tree is moving. A tree is killing. I hate trees," Hayat would say.

I knew that she meant the soldiers she saw in the news and how they used their green uniform to hide among trees. I did not want my daughter to hate nature, yet she was stubborn and insisted her visions were true. "I saw trees killing; I am sure, Mom."

It all happened a long time ago. Now my beautiful, little girl has become ashes glittering in the depth of my heart. I could not explain why I keep seeing her face in lavender, years after her death. It is a reminder of my mother who used to love those flowers. Sadly, my daughter and my mother were gathered in the same frame of loss. They are now the same distance away from me.

I did not know that the lavender was a sign. The lavender was a sign.

◊

After leaving my Salam's room, I went to the florist's in order to buy some lavender. I did not buy lavender that day; I only bought a small tree. When I put it next to Salam's desk, I whispered to my daughter fully certain she was there, "See, Hayat, it does not move."

◊

Home. This word suddenly rose in my mind as flashing fire. I felt colorless. I drank too much water until I became awfully united with my shadow. My shadow grew sadder and taller than me. My shadow never disappears, even in the midst of radiant light. Our home was lightly affected by a missile directed at a car passing our street. Only the windows shattered, and that was enough for history to repeat itself through a scar on Salam.

◊

When Salam and I left the hospital, we rented a new house, trying to make the best of the new situation and hoping that everything would be better. It was pale like a dead man, narrow like a grave. I wanted to take down all the mirrors before Salam had shouted, "No, leave them."

When he came closer to the mirror in the hall, he stood still like a palm tree. He never fell. His scar was more acceptable than mine. I brought a new small tree and put it in the new house. There I saw the troubled soul of my child. I whispered as I used to do since Hayat died, "See, it is still. No more killing."

◊

"It is your birthday. Wish something for your coming years," everybody shouted in one dense, unrecognized voice. I could only recognize that fading voice which came out of my son. I averted my eyes, looked around, and stumbled through all the faces in the room till they finally rested on his. He was standing like a scared bird, waving one wing and using the other to hide his scar. Both of us floated over the chaos, forming a separated world, like a bubble made up of light. I looked deeply into my son's eyes. Only he and I knew the secret wish. Seconds later, I was released of that world and said loudly, "I wished it."

◊

That night, I dreamed of Hayat holding a mirror for me. I was scarless. It was a hazy dream. When I got up, everything was dark except the moon, which looked like a radiant loaf of hope. For a moment, I imagined it falling. That upset me. I thought that I had forgotten that dream, yet unfortunately I did not. Things are recalled whenever they find the missing part.

"All people have scars, I swear," I told Salam one moonlit night.

"Have they all been through wars, mum?"

"Yes. Inner wars, darling."

He kept painting many drawings of people with scars. Some scars were on their hearts, others on their heads.

"Who is this?" I asked him.

"My father. You told me he did not have a hand."

◊

"How did you lose your hand?" I had asked my husband.

"I lost it. I was a little child spending a lot of time playing with other fellows. One day my arm was trapped in an opening made in some gate; behind it were hungry dogs. I did not know. I just wanted to open it; I couldn't even hear any barking that moment. See how unlucky I am! They bit my hand, turning it into a rotten piece of flesh. Terrified, I left it and ran."

I liked how he dramatized things. I laughed. No one loses his arm that way, I thought. But I suddenly realized that I did not care about the truth.

◊

I passed Salam's grave without uttering a word. It was August and the sun rose embracing the universe. I noticed the lavender growing dignifiedly over his grave. He died by a stray bullet that conquered his chest.

Sometimes I am surprised by the faith I still keep in my heart after all that happened. Nevertheless, all I want is to have God's forgiveness, for I really sometimes think that it was me who caused all of this for my beloved ones. It is said that the fire can destroy everything along its way for its own prosperity. Very often, I see a burning fire when I look at myself in the mirror, yet I do not want to believe that could be me.

Salam was left here, a red flower in blossom lying over a desert. I bent and closed his body towards my chest, allowing my scar to embrace his. I remember how I suddenly stopped when I had seen a falling moon embodied within him. It is not another war, for the first war which took away my family many years ago never ceased. They say wars end, but in fact, they never do. Wars never end.

◊

"Why do you want to keep it? It is a large, ugly, dark photo of a refugee woman. I don't even know why you insist on keeping it." He was referring to a photograph that hung beside the front door of the bleak house as if in holy status. Images were all we had at that house. No cameras, no fields—only dim light.

"It is a portrait from the Nakba, and we have to remember those people who went through so much agony. Furthermore, we have to pray that the coming generations can remember our agonies too, my son."

◊

"What is there beyond the sky?" I asked my mother.

"Paradise."

"What does it look like?"

"Like children's dreams."

I was afraid of telling my mother that I rarely dreamed. She would have thought I was a strange girl. I had a scattered childhood, but now I am piecing the puzzle together.

For some reason, I always imagined paradise like our green field, covered with a golden sun and a blue sky.

◊

"What is massacre, Mom?" Salam asked when I first told him what happened to my family.

"I do not know; maybe the survivors can never understand it. Only those who bled can answer you," I answered dramatically.

"But you bled too."

"All that I can tell you is that nothing can justify it, not even the most sacred ends in the world, not even peace itself, understand me?"

"Yes, Mom. Nothing can justify our scars."

I could not explain why I saw death in my son's eyes at that moment. The clouds came and attacked the moon later. No moon was seen in the heavens anymore.

◊

Now I am brought back home. I can still hear the echoes of my children everywhere I roam. The fields smell bloody and rotten, as if a hundred oxen were killed and thrown there. But they were not oxen. They were human bodies. It is war again which brought me back home, empty except for miserable memories.

I am only carrying bags of dazzling stars. They are heavy but useless, because they are not hung in the vast sky. I put the picture of the three of us everywhere. They were many; intentionally I would turn my face to a fixed direction. No pictures of me and Salam alone at all.

I kneeled in front of one of the big pictures in which we all looked happy and desolate at the same time. What a deceitful picture!

They did not like my daughter's name, and they took her to oppose its meaning. They were jealous of my son's name and took him to further a real one, a real kind of peace.

◊

"You are smiling."

"Yes, I am okay."

The first time Salam truly smiled was when he was dying.

This time there was no beautiful scene behind him, no more begging him to smile for the perfection of the scene, and no cameras. Nothing but a fading smile.

◊

The tree grew taller. Its leaves fell like devils' faces. I missed my son and my daughter. When I went to the florist's that day, I asked for some lavender.

"How many do you want, ma'am?"

"Many, so many please.... I want you to bring some to my home every day," I told him trying to hide my scar. For a second, I felt it was getting smaller. It almost vanished.

About the Writers

A note from Just World Books CEO
Helena Cobban

When we worked with Refaat Alareer to produce this anthology of short stories written in English by his students and mentees—and three that he contributed himself—we paid close attention to the section at the end of the book that provides brief biographies of the writers. He and we saw this as good chance to present to a global readership some of the powerful and engaging personal qualities of young people in Gaza who, as a group, had for far too long been systematically dehumanized in most Western media. The bios we presented in that 2013 edition were, as result, much fuller and more personal than in most such anthologies, and they retain their charm and poignancy until today, 2024.

In the aftermath of Refaat's assassination by the Israelis in December 2023, we decided to prepare this new Memorial Edition of *Gaza Writes Back*. After Refaat's killing, his friend and former student Dr. Yousef Aljamal, who had contributed a very moving story to the anthology, stepped forward to act as his literary executor. He and we are jointly committed to defending and extending Refaat's inspiring legacy as a writer and teacher as much as possible. With Yousef's help, in February 2024, we reached out to as many of the contributors to the 2013 edition as we could, to invite them to update their bios from the texts they had submitted at that time, and Yousef took on that assignment on his own account, as well.

Before we present the book's updated About the Writers section, here are a few notes:

1. Refaat Alareer was a man of grace, modesty, and good humor. In the 2013 edition, he urged that the short bio he submitted to this section be treated just like those of all the other story contributors. It was actually shorter in length than many of the other bios, and was presented second in that original list, which was organized alphabetically by the chosen transliteration of each writer's family name.

2. We and Yousef were unable to reach five of the 15 original story contributors. We assume that all or most of them are still trapped in Gaza and fear that some of them may already (like Refaat) be deceased. In compiling this section of the new 2024 edition, I decided to include here, in the same alphabetical order as in the first edition, both the new submissions we have from nine writers, which are labeled as "2024," and the earlier submissions we had from Refaat and the five other uncontactable writers, all labeled here as "2013." I feel that presenting these two sets of bios in their original order, but clearly labeled with the date of each, provides an intriguing window into some of the ways the lives of this cohort of young Palestinians have changed over the past eleven years.

3. I am deeply grateful to Yousef for his help in this matter, as many others, and to him and the other seven writers who amidst the turmoil they were experiencing in early 2024 on a relentless, continuing basis, took time out to write something deeply meaningful about the effect that Refaat Alareer had had on their lives. Two of these contributors—Nour El Borno and Dr. Ayah Rabah—sent us their new contributions from within Gaza. The others, including Yousef, sent theirs from the places on various continents to which their portion of the Gaza-Palestinian diaspora has for now been scattered.

Wafaa Abu Al-Qomboz

2013

Wafaa Abu Al-Qomboz is twenty-two years old and studying English at Islamic University in Gaza. She is a very proud Palestinian and Gazan. Since she was a young child, she used to hear many stories about Palestinian suffering due to the Israeli occupation and stories about Israeli soldiers attacking houses, killing children and women, and working very hard to destroy everything related to the identity of Palestinians. Wafaa lived the two wars on Gaza Strip: Cast Lead and Pillar of Cloud. She says, "Those two wars affected me significantly. I will not forget the sight of children who were mercilessly killed."

Wafaa was raised on the Palestinian values of tenacity and resisting injustice. Therefore, she started to think of something to help her defend her country and to let her express her frustration and anger at the occupation and to show her love to her country—writing. When she was eleven years old, Wafaa started writing simple short stories about Palestine and only recently she was encouraged to write in English. She is planning to continue writing in English.

Refaat Alareer

2013

A Cast Lead survivor, Refaat Alareer is an academic located in Gaza Strip. He finished his MA in Comparative Literature from the University College of London, and is currently doing his PhD in English Literature in Malaysia. Refaat has been teaching world literature, comparative literature, and creative writing since 2007.

He is currently interested in emerging Palestinian writers and works very closely with many of them in order to develop their creative writing and critical skills. That said, Refaat is the editor of *Gaza Writes Back*, a unique look, the first of its kind, at the struggle to a free Palestine: it is fiction, it is written by young Palestinians living in Gaza, and it is Gaza's creative way of reacting to Israel's aggression that culminated in what was called Operation Cast Lead. The book is an attempt to expose the atrocities of all occupations, as well as their violations of all basic human rights.

In his own words: *Palestine was first occupied metaphorically, i.e. in words and stories and poems. So, we ought to write back, to use all efforts and pens, and promote our cause to educate both ourselves and all the peoples of the world about our cause. Telling our own tales is resistance—resistance to forgetfulness and to occupation. Resistance is making noise, and as Malcolm X put it, "If you want something, you had better make some noise."*

Jehan Alfarra

2013

Jehan Alfarra is a twenty-four-year-old blogger and a multi-media activist from the Gaza Strip. Jehan advocates the Palestinian cause and the reality of life in Gaza through social media and various multi-media outlets, by collaborating with international and local organizations.

Jehan was a Youth Council Member at the Mercy Corps' GCC (Global Citizen Corps) program, where she joined her first blogging team, Beyond Our Borders. Jehan now runs her own blog and is one of the founding members of Diwan Ghazza, a cultural forum in Gaza. She was a member of the Palestinian Youth Advocacy Network (PYAN) at the House of Wisdom in Gaza, where she was also a member of the delegations' reception protocol. Much of Jehan's work with international and local organizations involves English language training, interpretation, and translation of both English and Arabic.

Jehan is telling the story of Palestine, the story that stems from the world of tents and is marked by nights of hunger, darkness, and fear; the story of children; the story that lives on hopes of self-determination and has survived years and years of misery, agony, and tears, replacing them with echoing laughter and lively smiles; the story of episodes of pain repeated one day after another and yet faced with incredibly strong, light-spirited hearts; the story of a pen that never seems to run out of ink; the story of what F-16 Jets, Apaches, Merkava tanks, and machine guns do; the story of stones lying on the banks of the land; the story of an exceptional instinct for survival despite despair and ultimate injustice; the story of a place that used

2024

In Memory of Refaat Alareer

Long before he became my teacher and mentor, Refaat was simply the humorous young man I had met at the border as he tried to make his way to London to pursue a masters degree.

It was 2006. I was a young student selected to go study at an American high school as part of an exchange program. Along with a group of other high school students from Gaza, I made the trip to the infamous Rafah Crossing, hoping to travel to the United States for the first time. This stranger was there with us, trying to leave Gaza as well.

As we waited outside the border gates, there was plenty of time for jokes and conversation. He would playfully fight us over our US State Department–sponsored baseball caps, the only thing shielding us from the blazing sun. As we all laughed and cracked jokes together, his sarcasm was distinctive!

Hours would pass, only for us all to be turned away and told to come back and try again the following day...and then the day after that, and the day after that. It felt like such an impossible mission to be able to make it out. At the end of each day, Refaat would smile and say, "See you kids tomorrow." We made a bit of an acquaintance in our relentless quest to break free.

We had to return to the border so many times that we stopped saying a proper goodbye to our families. The first time I left my family for the border, I cried; I was meant to go away for an entire year, alone. The second day, there were no tears. Every time after that, I would just laugh and say, "See you later tonight!"

There was this measure of hopelessness and acceptance that we were "trapped," a sense of almost certainty we were not going to make it out of Gaza, that we would all be back home by nightfall after every single attempt. And yet there was still this constant hope we will somehow make it through, sending us to the border again and again. This hope and hopelessness, at odds yet always married and intertwined, have encapsulated so much of our lives and our experiences as Palestinians.

In Gaza, under the rainfall of Israeli bombs, Gazans are mired in hope and hopelessness. They accept death with a sense of almost certainty that they are next, but with every day there is also an undying hope lurking underneath that they will somehow still survive.

In 2006, Refaat and I made it out of Gaza, but not everyone at the border did. In Gaza today, not everyone will survive, but what Refaat has taught me over the years is that their stories and their memories will live forever. And it is on us to tell their tales, to keep them and their hopes alive.

This time, Refaat has not made it out, but his will always be a tale to tell. And even in the darkest hours, it will always bring hope.

Sarah Ali

2013

Sarah Ali, a Palestinian born in Kuwait in 1991, is a resident of Gaza and grew up in Gaza City. In 2009, she joined the Faculty of Arts at the Islamic University of Gaza (IUG) and graduated in 2013 with a bachelor's degree in English Language and Literature. Currently, Sarah works as an English language teacher and trainer. She is interested in many things, including literature, literary criticism, linguistics, art, nature, politics, religion, and interfaith studies. She specifically focuses on postcolonial literature, the relationship between the colonizers and the colonized, and the representation of the self and the other. Issues of identity and self-doubts are also of interest to her.

Sarah started writing in Arabic at an early age, but only after the 2008–9 offensive Israel launched against the Gaza Strip has she started to write in English. Having majored in and studied literature, Sarah believes in the power of writing. To her, fighting and resisting occupation happen on different fronts, not least in areas of journalism and media.

Furthermore, she thinks young bloggers/writers in Palestine and other occupied territories should have the opportunity to speak for themselves and to voice opinions long silenced or neglected. In Sarah's view, challenging and ultimately changing stereotypical images circulated and accepted about who Palestinians are and what they stand for is part of Palestinian writers' mission. Sarah supports Palestinian resistance in all its forms and advocates one state for its entire people, regardless of their race or religion.

In her own words: *Writing is both a way of self-expression and a way of spreading the word and revealing the truth about the injustice done to the Palestinian people.*

2024

After my graduation from Islamic University of Gaza's English Department in 2013, I worked as a teaching assistant there for one year before pursuing a master's degree in English Literary Studies at Durham University, UK (2014-2015). I then went home and worked as a lecturer of English Literature at IUG for four years. At the end of 2019, I started a PhD in English Literature at Cambridge University.

I cannot think of a stage of my education or career since 2013, or indeed since I was fifteen years old, when I first met Refaat, that was not influenced by his wisdom, guidance, and incredible support. He ran an English Language and Literature Forum called "Eye on Palestine" for about a decade before it shut down in 2010. It was an innovative and interactive forum that helped young Palestinians in Gaza connect with the outside world long before social media became popular. We wrote stories and discussed poetry and sought joy in learning the nuances of English grammar. Some of the pieces submitted to the forum went on to inspire stories that later became part of *Gaza Writes Back*.

It was such a pleasure to work with Refaat on *Gaza Writes Back*, and I am humbled to be credited in his acknowledgements to the book: I was there from day one; I suggested texts, read them, and worked with Refaat and the writers to give the stories the form and shape they now have. I was a recent graduate at the time. In addition to being a fantastic reader and editor, Refaat was incredibly down to earth. Seeing his humility up close as he collaborated with students and took their suggestions in the most earnest manner inspired great trust and respect.

A couple years later, we were working together again, this time at IUG, teaching English Literature at the Faculty of Arts. Those were years of thoughtful insights and endless joy: I worked closely with Refaat, got to know him better as a colleague, and we sometimes taught the same modules (Comparative Literature, Romanticism, Victorian Literature). There is an amazing side to having Refaat as a workmate. Apart from the sheer joy of his humor, the snack-sharing, and the cheesy puns (the worse the puns were, the better), Refaat was an incredibly generous friend and colleague, always sharing resources and recommending books. Nobody I know dissected a poem, and then sewed it back together into a perfect whole, as Refaat did. You could listen to him read poetry and explain poetry and breathe poetry for hours on end! Refaat's passion, his integrity at work, and his devotion to his students made my own experience of teaching much more worthwhile. We organised seminars together, wrote examinations, hosted speakers, redesigned departmental study plans, and worked on annual shows for the English Department. Refaat's knowledge, his brilliant guidance, and his sharp intellect defied the Israeli-imposed intellectual blockade on Palestinian students in Gaza; he helped create an environment that nourished curious minds and encouraged budding talents to thrive.

Embarking on a PhD was not an easy decision for me to make. Not only did Refaat encourage me to apply, but he supported me every step of the way, wrote my recommendation letter for Cambridge, and guided me throughout the process. In the darkest phases of PhD mental breakdowns, he offered his writing tips with patience and care that truly inspired. Some of our most recent conversations, even during Israel's ongoing genocide in Gaza, were about courses he believed we could potentially co-teach at IUG once I finished my PhD and went home. When my father passed away in Gaza in December 2022, I was unable to be with my family because of the Israeli-Egyptian siege. Refaat was at my father's funeral on the first day. His kindness, his compassion, and his enormous heart were remarkable.

It is cruel to write about a close friend's passing, but if there is anything we learned from Refaat's legacy, it is that he would not want us to wallow in grief when there is a story to tell. It is for Refaat's story, for the tale that brings hope, that we carry on.

Yousef Aljamal

2013

Yousef Aljamal is a twenty-four-year-old graduate from the Islamic University in Gaza and is currently doing his MA at the University of Malaya in Malaysia. In the past two years, Yousef translated hundreds of articles, studies, and reports on Palestine from Western media outlets. Yousef is a blogger committed to promoting the Palestinian narrative in the West through translation and recently co-translated *The Prisoners' Diaries*, a compilation of twenty-two Palestinian prisoners' experiences in Israeli jails.

Yousef believes strongly in alternative media to reach the masses in the world, in a time when mainstream media is biased against Palestinians and very supportive of their oppressors.

Yousef started writing in 2010, in a time when the siege imposed on Gaza was very tight. His first piece during the time of the siege got published, and he received encouragement from his classmates and teachers. For Yousef, to write is to exist.

In his own words: *In today's world, words might be stronger than war machines and sharper than swords. To write is to tell the story, and stories make it now, eternal, and forever. To write is to re-own my story. To write is to keep memory fresh, lest we forget, lest details vanish as time passes.*

I prefer to write about my personal experience under occupation, for it relates more to people outside. Owning and reclaiming Palestinian narrative by Palestinians is my top priority for the next period of time. "Until Lions have their own historian, the history of the hunt will glorify the hunter," as Chenua Achebe put it.

2024

Refaat Changed Our lives

Refaat was the one who taught me and many others the love of writing and storytelling. It is hard to write about him. I never thought that I would have to tell Refaat's story, as he requested in his poem "If I Must Die," so that his death brings hope and becomes a tale. Refaat was a man of love and joy; he always brought laughter and positive energy to our life, using his wit and ability to shape language the way he wanted.

In 2013, I was on the same flight as Refaat, traveling to Malaysia to finish our post-graduate studies. When he figured out I had no plans yet for my accommodation, he invited me to stay with him. I slept in his living room for about three weeks. I felt heartbroken as I carried out my luggage to my new place. He was more than a teacher for us. He was our guide and mentor.

He had the darkest humor too. When I had dinner at a friend's house a couple of days after leaving his place, he called me to tell me I was ungrateful, because I didn't compliment the food I'd been provided during my three-week stay. He told me he would "burn me" for my ingratitude—and he asked me to come and offer an apology to him and his flatmates, Housam and Mohammed. (Mohammed was killed in an airstrike a few days after Refaat was killed.) I brought a watermelon and we had a good reconciliation. After that, we got closer and I would spend the weekend at his place for the two years I stayed in Malaysia.

Mohammed would always say I acted just like Refaat, because Refaat would not tolerate a typo or an incorrect punctuation mark. I felt proud that, after attending Refaat's classes back in Gaza, I later became one of his close friends. We launched the Malaysian version of *Gaza Writes Back* together. We spoke and we traveled to other cities in Malaysia together. After one talk, a man stepped up and purchased 50 copies of *Gaza Writes Back* after he heard Refaat speak! During those travels, I came to understand that Refaat was the greatest of all the people I met in my life.

Refaat was universal in his knowledge, class, and connections. He was known to many young people in Gaza as he trained hundreds of them on creative writing and storytelling. I had the honor to help him set up some of those workshops.

He was also known to many people outside Gaza through his activism on X and the many interviews he made from Gaza. He chose to stay close to Shujayia in the north of Gaza and tell the stories of people there. During the genocide, every day he would walk 25,000 steps to connect to the internet. He remained true to his principles and beliefs. That was no surprise, as he was inspired in his life by people like Malcom X—as he had told the assessors in the interview he did for a Fulbright Scholarship. (He won that scholarship to do his Ph.D. in the United States. Israel denied him a permit to leave Gaza for that purpose. But later, he was able to win his Ph.D. at the University of Malaya.)

In 2014, Just World Books and the American Friends Service Committee organized a speaking tour that took Refaat, my colleague Rawan Yaghi, and me to more than a dozen cities around the United States. He said that meeting Jewish Americans and seeing Jews who, for the first time, were not pointing a gun at him was his "Malcom X moment."

During the speaking tour, Refaat was able to influence many people, moving some of them to tears. He believed in the power of storytelling and made each one of his students believe that she or he had a story that deserved to be told. He empowered a lot of people and only later in his life did he start to tell his own story.

Ustaz (teacher) Refaat was full of life. He would carry a book under his elbow and was always running to yet another workshop, talk, or adventure. He left his footprints everywhere he went. From Washington, DC, where he has an armchair at Helena Cobban's place named after him, to Melaka, Malaysia, where he saw two identical cats and promptly named them Copy and Paste, he always left a mark. He introduced the U.S. to his beloved town of Shujaiya, calling Chicago the Shujaiya of the U.S. and calling New York the Zaytoun of the U.S., since

Zayotun and Shujaiya have a rivalry similar to that between the two American cities.

Refaat highlighted the importance of fighting against the intellectual isolation of the Palestinians in Gaza. He called for more students from there to travel and learn, and then to return to Gaza—which was what he himself did upon finishing his PhD in 2017. Refaat was able to touch so many hearts! I would not be here in Istanbul today were it not for Refaat who supported me through my studies for first my MA, then my Ph.D. When I finally gained my doctorate, I called him and he was thrilled to learn I had finally finished. He never said no when I invited him to speak to young people here too.

Refaat changed my life and those of so many of his other students for the better. He was Gaza's storyteller but also our big brother, who would check on us years after we left Gaza, or would visit our families to check on them while we were away. He was always there for us; he was always there for Gaza.

When I visited Bellingham in the U.S. in October 2023, he asked me to check on a computer mouse he left at a friend's house, saying there must be at least 1,000 mice there now. To the last day of his life, and when Israel's bombs poured into Gaza like rain, he kept his sense of humor and his humanity. He fed the street cats. He told people's stories. And he cracked one joke after another, to the extent that his followers on X asked him how could he keep this sense of humor amidst the genocide.

I will always be thankful that our paths crossed, Refaat, and it is the thing that I am proudest of, that I can say I am a student of yours. Your seeds will continue to multiply. You always come back, Refaat. You always do.

Nour Al-Sousi

2013

Nour Al-Sousi has survived a loss of a country, two wars, and some twenty-five years. Nour finished her BA in English Language and Literature from the Islamic University of Gaza. Reading and writing were Nour's passion since she was a young child. Since then, writing became second nature, something like breathing. The composition classes were her favorite, and nothing has ever pleased her more than that look of admiration in the teachers' eyes after reading a piece or a story she had written.

Nour won an online contest for a short story she wrote early in her writing career and thus was encouraged by many to start her own blog.

Living in Palestine, particularly in Gaza, is Nour's source of inspiration, and her writings mainly express what Palestinians experience in their daily life. Being a Gazan Palestinian has taught her that one can resist not only by guns, but also by words. Now, Nour is an English teacher. She tries to teach her students the power of words.

In her own words: *As the second Intifada broke out in September 2000, I started to understand how our life, as Palestinians, is a struggle. In such a struggle, I had nothing but my pen to hold, so I wrote several short stories about martyrs who were my age.*

Shahd Awadallah

2013

Shahd Awadallah is a twenty-four-year-old graduate of the Islamic University of Gaza, English Department. Shahd works as an English teacher in an UNRWA school in Gaza. Since she started reading at the age of seven, fiction has become her passionate interest. Her journey with writing started at the age of eighteen, when she was a secondary school student. Writing was Shahd's enjoyable pastime and her way of relaxing.

Shahd writes about people whose smiles and tears tell a lot about their lives and circumstances. In addition, living in a country under occupation, Palestine, affected what and how she writes.

In her own words: *Expressing my own experiences and others' stories, exposing what I go through as unseen stories or crimes created or committed by the Israeli occupier, all of this helped me know more, be stronger, be more aware of my own case and convey these images and realities to the rest of the world by writing short stories.*

Nour El Borno

2013

Nour El Borno is twenty years old. She studies English Literature at the Islamic University of Gaza. Nour is addicted to writing, movies, and reading, and she wishes to become an English teacher. Nour started writing English poetry when she was in high school. Poetry, for her, is the oxygen she breathes, her way out.

In her own words: *The difference between the old me and the new me is the source of inspiration. I used to be inspired by friends and family. However, now I am mainly inspired by nature. I started to believe that if a person can write effectively, it is his or her duty to get up, write, and help change this world to something better, and that's what I am doing or trying to do.*

I hope one day this world will be safe and better for all generations. I do believe that my cause, full of wars and suffering, could be assisted by writing. Maybe one day, our writings will be a path for our freedom. Therefore, I decided that if my writing will affect only one person, then that's a huge thing.

2024

To the Better Craftsman

The Daffodils yet await your arrival,
"When will he come?" they wonder.
The words line up in symmetry—and wait:
How long will it be until his next lecture?

The door handle of room N four hundred and two
Feels nostalgic to your forceful entrance.
Forceful yet graceful—something about you
Makes a real difference.

"No one enters late," you make a statement,
But sometimes, when needed, show forgiveness.
A dream you had: creativity and discipline—
Everyone can write a poem.
Everyone can be a storyteller.

Then Heaven's eye casts its rays on the board
And asks, noticing your absence,
"Why not today? Where is Mr. Refaat?"
            Silly me—you then became Doctor Refaat.

We met in 2008—you were a young man;
Filled with passion and enthusiasm.
Nothing changed in 2012
When you became my university teacher.

Something in your air makes the room glow,
It must have been your love for literature.
Read—Read—Read:
Your, forever, motto.
"Don't quote," you quote, to teach us be ourselves;
Funny and ironic—quite often, cynical.

"Refaat?" Hamlet asks, "Mother, have you seen him?"
She stutters. He recently lost his father,
Can he, now, lose a friend so dear?

"Thou art to grieve, more,
Thou art to be in woe, for long;

And black shall be the colour of your cloak
For many years to go".

"Tis not alone my inky cloak, good mother, Nor customary suits
of solemn black, Nor windy suspiration of forced breath, No,
nor the fruitful river in the eye, Nor the dejected 'havior of the
visage, Together with all forms, moods, shapes of grief, That can
denote me truly".

On a fearful night—with owls screaming loud
An airstrike hits Refaat's refuge.
Under the rubble he so often wrote about,
Remains his residue.
His memories.
His poems.
His students.
His classes.
His characters.
Beowulf—tried to rescue him—
But he too died in him.
Refaat was killed—yet:

His children live to tell his stories,
His students take on his journey;
His poems—touch more hearts,
And his books breathe his legacy.

And mark my words and remember:

So long as men can breathe or eyes can see,
—Dear Refaat—
So long lives this and this gives life to thee.

Adieu.

Hanan Habashi

2013

Hanan Habashi was born in Gaza in 1990. She studied English Literature at the Islamic University of Gaza (IUG) and currently works as an English Language trainer and a translator. Hanan is interested in music, languages, literature, and folklore of all kinds. Hanan believes that the Palestinian youth are capable of fighting for their just cause against the Israeli occupation on all fronts. She believes in the constructive power of the spoken and written word. The first writing she did was when she started a diary on the fourth day of the Cast Lead Operation (2008–2009) in the form of a death note, in what first sounded to her as a desperate scream down an empty street. By writing her first short story, "L for Life," Hanan had her first empowering writing experience. She later came to the belief that Palestine—the land, the people, and the memories—must not be funneled through the narrow concept of a "conflict between two."

Writing Palestine, Hanan thinks, is the responsibility of Palestinians—nobody else's. Being the stateless, dispossessed people they are, telling the story of the land is the first step for Palestinians on their road to self-determination. Ghassan Kanafani is Hanan's writing role model. Some more intellectuals like Kanafani might not set Palestine free, but they will absolutely "knock the walls of the tank."

In her own words: *Because many people around the world think they have the right to speak on their behalf, Palestinians are suffering two opposing stereotypical images that are equally disturbing and doing the just cause injustice: the Palestinian as a helpless victim, a mere object of sympathy, or as a bloodthirsty savage. Palestinians are neither.*

2024

I am an English Language instructor with over a decade of experience now, driven by a deep passion for bridging language barriers and fostering genuine connections. My journey, supported by an MA in TESOL and Applied Linguistics, has allowed me to blend academic writing and reading with creative expression. Though I don't see myself as a writer, my love for creative writing has been profoundly shaped by Dr. Refaat Alareer. As my teacher and the first person who truly believed in my storytelling potential, his encouragement and constant support has been a guiding light for me. Inspired by him, I had the honor of co-creating the Paper Boats Zine, a project that celebrated the voices of women from Gaza and highlighted the rich, diverse tapestry of our community.

I strive to create safe spaces for underprivileged communities, including through reading and writing clubs that offer platforms for marginalized voices. Writing has always provided refuge and perspective, but now, I feel a deep sense of responsibility to continue Dr. Refaat's legacy by fostering authentic storytelling and pushing against dominating narratives.

By the way, after Dr. Refaat's martyrdom, I felt a deep and personal urge to share my voice publicly, an urge all his students and friends deeply felt. I started to write publicly on @hanan-rights, a tiny Instagram account with raw pieces of writing attempts. I think this is the Refaat Effect, far subtler and more powerful than the butterfly effect.

Tasnim Hammouda

2013

Tasnim Hammouda is a nineteen-year-old Palestinian student living in Gaza City. A lot of her passion for English language is derived from her mother, who was her English teacher. Born to a dedicated mother who would always support her children to do their best, Tasnim quickly found herself on the right path to improve her English skills. "The future belongs to those who prepare for it now," her favorite quote of Malcolm X, would always come as an answer to what her life motto is. She believes in it and has her mind and heart set on a plan where her academic life and English major come first.

When she was fourteen, Tasnim joined an advanced English language course. It was everything a life-changing experience can be. Surrounded by the right teacher and opportunities, she started writing in English. Then the first war on Gaza took place. Along with many Gazans, it took Tasnim a while to pull herself together and go on after such a painful time, when she almost lost her parents and house to an Israeli bomb. Tasnim, more decisive than ever before, insisted to be a more tangible presence in her community. One thing the war has taught her to do was to see her society as a whole of which she is an essential part. She grew up and so did her dreams. Her latest endeavor to learn more was on June 20th, 2013, when she traveled to the United States as part of a leadership program. During her six-week-long stay there, she was exposed to new writing styles, and she got a step closer to achieving her future goals.

In her own words: *Only then [during the advanced English course] did I realize that mastering English could be much more than just a future major. It was an expressive way to be more creative in a world where words are significantly mighty.*

Elham Hilles

2013

Born in 1988, Elham Hilles is a Palestinian inhabitant of Gaza City. She finished high school in 2006 and then joined the Islamic University of Gaza to study English Literature, which she had dreamed of since she was young. Elham is married and is a full-time homemaker. Elham's main interests are translation, Arabic and Russian literature, comparative literature, and politics. Before writing in English, she wrote many Arabic satirical topics and short stories for online forums from 2007 to 2009.

Elham considers writing as a means of escape, a way to contemplate the world around her and to create something out of nothing through words.

In her own words: *Writing is a way of resistance through which I attempt to highlight the distress and agony of the Palestinian refugees in the wretched camps around my city.*

Samiha Olwan

2013

Samiha Olwan, twenty-five years old, is an MA graduate of Cultural Studies from Durham University, United Kingdom, and an English Literature graduate from the Islamic University of Gaza. Sameeha started her own blog several years ago after the end of the Gaza war, also known as Operation Cast Lead (2008–9). Her entrapment in an intense situation of life and death reflected how imprisoned she was in a whole national struggle to which individual and collective identity was already objectified and fixed. Sameeha writes because of the inevitability of writing back to a discourse that dehumanized Palestinians' whole existence and a victim narrative that subjected them to the interpretations of what their life should look like and how it should be presented. She faced that with her own voice, a Palestinian voice.

For Sameeha, every experience lived is an experience worth recording, and each of those now "told" tales—whether they stem from a genuine experience, the representation of experiences of others, or those experiences enshrined in Palestinians by the virtue of being Palestinians, like displacement and return—are worth remembering and telling. Memory in itself is the only thing that is left of their comprehension of home and identity. Both the word and the virtual space that made them both readable and accessible have been their "soft weapons."

In her own words: *Speaking of the "I" that is "myself" and reflecting on my own individual situation was the main reason why I started my blog. And I uttered my voice through the pages of virtual space where the fragmentation of home and identity found a unifying space in which my voice was not restricted by the conventions of autobiographical writing as a classic genre, but was rather liberated by the voice of the "I" and the genuine experience lived under occupied fragmented spaces.*

2024

The very first time I walked into his Shakespeare class, encouraged by a friend in her senior year, Mr. Refaat was welcoming and did not mind the first-year intruder. As an English literature student, I never missed any of Mr. Refaat's classes after that. Sometimes, I even took the same class twice. For those of us passionate about literature, something about Mr. Refaat's enthusiasm for literature has always stayed with us.

"If you prick us, do we not bleed? If you tickle us, do we not laugh? If you poison us, do we not die?" He would recite Shylock's soliloquies, walking up and down the lecture hall, the tone of his voice mixing emphasis with passion, and his eyes roaming the room for those of us with signs of curiosity, those of us who shared his passion for the aesthetics of literature.

His class on the metaphysical poets and John Donne's conceits and extended metaphors was an extension of his joyful intellect. As he lectured us on how the metaphysicals reasoned with poetry, he'd emphasize, "It is the 'how,' Samiha, not the 'what,' of we are saying that matters."

Mr Refaat celebrated our little triumphs over form with such pride. "Did you intentionally leave that blank space to denote silencing? Brilliant, Samiha," he'd casually congratulate me and I would fly with happiness.

His fascination with English literature, with figures like Shakespeare, Blak,e and T.S. Eliot, was not uncritical, however. Amidst our study of the canon, he made sure to hand us copies of Malcom X's autobiography, of Sartre's introduction to Fanon's *The Wretched of the Earth* and taught us to search for the subaltern amidst the canon. We spent hours speculating the ways we are depicted in canonised literature, and further hours unlearning the fear to challenge, question, and disrupt their authority.

Mr. Refaat was also our introduction to a broad array of Palestinian literature, a body of work that was otherwise side-lined by the department's conventional and traditional English literature program. His pigeonhole at his office was a library on loan, and the books he collected during his Masters studies in the UK were always available for students to borrow. We'd casually pick books from that pigeonhole every week. If he was in the office, we'd have extensive conversations about those books. It was a secret book club of sorts.

Mr. Refaat saw the rich fund of talent in Gaza society. He taught us to rebel against the image of the abject victim and to challenge simplistic portrayals of our stories as Palestinian youth grappling with a life under occupation. Before he officially created the "We are Not Numbers" writing group, he often held free writing workshops with Palestinian youth.

And while he mastered the political rhetoric and could speak eloquently and extensively on settler colonialism, ethnic cleansing, and the inhumane and illegal blockade, and about the daily violations of human rights that Palestinians experience, his passion was in the stories that lay buried under the rubble, the voices (though loud and clear) that were silenced behind besieged walls and deafening bombs. He listened attentively for these stories, and held a space for them, and he emphasized for us again and again that they do matter.

Mr. Refaat was a visionary, a soul that never tired of giving. He was not just a brilliant academic. For many of his students, he was much more.

To see his last poem cited everywhere is sometimes painful, because this poem only touches the surface of what Mr Refaat meant to us, and what he was. If he was celebrated while alive, I can imagine his pride, while he continued to work and listen with humility.

Mr Refaat, we are sorry that all our tributes fall short of explaining the pain of your loss, but so far, we are not given the chance to grieve the inhumane toll of loss amidst an ongoing genocide. May you Rest in Power.

◊

Samiha Olwan graduated from the Islamic University of Gaza in 2010 and worked as a teaching assistant there, 2010-2011. She is now a lecturer of English Literature and Creative Writing at Murdoch University, Western Australia, with a PhD in English and Comparative Literature. Her PhD research explored the gendered voice in Palestinian women bloggers' narratives. Her interest in those narratives was sparked in 2010 when she started blogging about her life in Gaza under the Israeli blockade, and developed further as she worked with the Palestinian Centre for Human Rights (PCHR) to document women's accounts of Israeli aggressions in the Gaza Strip. Through her scholarly work, she hopes she can bring more stories of women from the periphery to the centre. Samiha was a student of Refaat, a colleague, and a friend.

Ayah Rabah

2013

Aya Rabah is a twenty-year-old medical student at Al-Azhar University in Gaza. She frequently does volunteer work with the Medical Students' Association, yet nothing seems sufficient for someone who wants to spend her life working for others. To Aya, writing is the most brilliant thing that makes her feel accomplished and provides her with more reasons to carry on. Aya reacted to the scenes of death in the second Palestinian Intifada by writing, and she reacted to the Cast Lead war on Gaza by even more writing.

The first things that provoked Aya to write were the bittersweet memories about Palestine and Palestinian heroes. Like many Palestinians, Aya was haunted, and equally inspired, by the prisoners, the martyrs, the several generations of refugees, and images of stolen lands, wars, death, and destruction Israel brought on Palestine.

In her own words: *Studying medicine in Gaza, I could see half of my dream coming true, while the rest is kept so far and embodied in the bodies of patients whom I am going to heal or even in the words I am going to write. I came to realize that writing is the most magnificent meaning of freedom.... I found my way out through writing. When I write, I feel my life is devoted to greater goals and when I do so, I feel I am the person I want to be. Writing keeps me in a struggle for existence and is a meaningful justification to survive.*

2024

It was the night of my fifteenth birthday. I still remember vividly how I sat for hours trying hard to write my first English story as a remarkable beginning of my new year—before it turned midnight. The next day would be the day of my weekly English lessons with my best teacher, Mr. Refaat, and all I wanted was to give him my first story.

Days passed. I felt so impatient for next week's lesson, when I might hear his reaction to my first attempt. He entered the classroom with his unforgettable serene and noble presence and before the lesson began, he turned his face towards me and said that he was impressed by the story and I should continue to write. I can still recall the sweet turbulence in my heart and the flush of dreams but more importantly the happiness, really pure happiness and pride, that I felt upon his compliment on the first literary work of a child who was still seeking her identity in the Gaza that was her entire world.

During the first war in Gaza in 2008, we had to stop the lectures and stay at home. Because of this teacher, I had survived this war having my pen and my notebook beside me and I kept writing and ignoring the madness of war outside. I wrote stories about it all and felt strong, resilient, and thankful.

The first time we met after that war was unforgettable. He was sitting in front of us reading a part of Tamim Albargouthi's poem loudly: "I would sacrifice myself for every sad Victor, whose beloved ones were killed while trying to protect the others!" And then he stopped trying hard to hide his tears. In a moment, everything turned into tears in the room: the walls, the sun's rays as they rested on his beautiful face and even that heavy silence that seemed unbreakable back then.

Years went on and I did not see Mr. Refaat after the scholarship program to learn English came to its end, but I always deeply cherished the memories I had of working with him. Later, in 2013, I received his invitation to contribute to a book telling stories about the war in Gaza. I was charged with emotions to prove to him again what he taught us for such a long time. After sending my story, I waited with stress for his answer. I was studying medicine and continued to write from time to time. Oh, Mr Refaat, if I could see him one more time, just to tell him that I remember every single word he said to me as he was holding my story's draft, making comments as we met in a building that was bombed during this ongoing war of 2023. I was happy that I fulfilled his expectations.

I became a medical doctor, and I still try to tell our stories as Palestinians, just as he wanted us to do. I also published my first novel in Arabic in 2020, *Because Love Never Fades Away.*

I did not and I still cannot believe the passing away of my best-ever teacher who taught me to rise up from pain and transform it into words that others can read, repeat, and hopefully interact with. I owe him the biggest gratitude in my life and he will have till the last word I write in my life my respect, love, and deep thanks.

Rest in power, my beloved teacher, and may your words live forever!

Mohammed Suliman

2013

Mohammed Suliman is a Gaza-based writer and human rights worker. He obtained a master's degree in human rights from the London School of Economics. His writing has appeared on different online publications, including Al Jazeera English, Open Democracy, the *Electronic Intifada*, and *Mondoweiss*.

Because he has lived most of his life in a region characterized by political turbulence, instability, and violence, resulting from the Israeli occupation of the Palestinian people and their land, Mohammed found himself obliged to record his views, experiences, and diaries as he witnesses them first-hand. Mohammed created a blog so that people can read and become more familiar with the lives of Palestinians away from the illusively complex political speeches and enigmatic media analyses. People who have never been to Gaza mostly form an image of life in Palestine, in Gaza particularly, as full of misery and suffering where there is no room for a peaceful moment to live. Mohammed's blog, however, talks of peace as well as war, of hope as well as despair, of displacement as well as the inevitability of return. Mohammed writes about, for, and to Gaza and its people.

In his own words: *The very word [Gaza] is evocative of a whole lot of irreconcilable senses: of life and death, of delight and misery, of excitement and wretchedness, of hopefulness and despair, of Hamas and Fateh. Gaza, the word, by its own nature, and upon the mere pronunciation of it, automatically conjures up two images deeply inculcated in the memory of every Gazan: one of Fares Oda, unflinchingly facing a tank and throwing a stone at it, and the other of Mohammed El-Dorra, embraced by his father, and crying for his life. The word, although light as it seems, weighs heavily upon the heart of its enemies.*

2024

Even in the midst of omnipresent death, even when one becomes closely familiar with the spectacle of mass death, when the chances of dying are greater than living, when death becomes an ominous but all too reliable friend, even in war, in genocide, in Gaza, when the thought of death is the most constant thought, and the smell of death the most palpable smell, and the reality of death is the most potent reality, even then, when death is the most frequent visitor, and the most common wanderer, and the most intimate confidant, even when everyone dies, when everyone anticipates death in any instance, when peril is the condition of existence, and all are expected to die, even then, there are certain persons who do *not* die. Even then, there are persons who must survive. Our minds simply cannot conceive of the possibility of the death of such a person, of such a figure, of such a symbol. The death of this individual threatens the collective existence of the whole people. It is excommunicated from the realm of the possible and lies entirely outside the consciousness of the living. This type of person must be protected. This type of person cannot die.

Or can they?

Perhaps, then, I ought to say Refaat's "passing away" or Refaat's "departure from this life," rather than his "death" because Refaat cannot be allowed to die. But no euphemism will help to soften the reality of Refaat's death. Refaat has died. But Refaat did not just die. How abominable he would have found the neutralization of his death as "mere" death. Refaat was *murdered*. He was murdered by the Israeli state, which murdered a great many of his family members—his sister, his brother, his nephews, his nieces, his in-laws, and many more—the state which destroyed his home, obliterated his neighbourhood, annihilated his city, uprooted his people, orphaned his children, and which has committed so many dangerous crimes against the humanity of Refaat and of his people. Refaat was not protected. He was allowed to be murdered.

A person such as described above did not exist, then, except as a figment of our imagination. Such a figure, such an invincible hero, only existed in our helpless minds faced with the ubiquity of the Israeli death machine. Everyone on the receiving end of the Israeli murder machine is vulnerable, most of all the defenceless civilians, even those who fight against oppression with words, even intellectuals, thoughtful people, writers, poets, inspirational leaders of civil resistance movements, coming face to face with the Israeli state, even they will be hunted down by the Israeli military, even if from the air, and they will be murdered. In Gaza, everyone dies; everyone is murdered, and no one—*no one*—is protected.

The death of such a person must then be violent. More violent than murder. More violent than bombs and airstrikes. More violent than physical violence. The murder of such an individual is an irrevocably scarring event. For with the murder of someone like Refaat, all humanity must come to terms with the possibility of murder—of being murdered, with no consequences for the murderer. It is a horrifying confrontation with the most vicious of realities: the reality of genocide, and of the murder of one who had hitherto been thought to be immune from murder, from barbarity, to be protected even—and specially—in genocide. The death—the murder—of this individual must contravene all laws, all norms, all thoughts, and all expectations. Everyone can die, then. There are no protected persons in war, in genocide, in Gaza. Everyone can be murdered, and Refaat is no exception.

But Refaat was an exception. I met Refaat in my first undergraduate class as a student of English at the Islamic University of Gaza. He was a *cool* teacher: energetic, inspiring, and entertaining. He possessed an encyclopedic knowledge of English and world literature. He led by example. His compassion for others was limitless. His humility was most sincere. He never treated students as subordinates but as equals: he elevated them to his level. He treated them as though they were all his younger brothers. He was a restless thinker, pacing up and down the classroom, asking punctilious questions about what seemed to be the most insignificant details in this Shakespearean play or that Dickensian novel, and after allowing a moment of awkward silence, he would answer the questions himself, as though muttering to himself, lost in a monologue, and experimenting with his own ideas, testing his own logic, before his awestruck students.

Refaat inculcated in his students the love of writing and of storytelling. Against the background of occupation, blockade, bombing, invasion, and strife, mediocrity had become the ceiling of the hopes and aspirations of a generation of young university students and graduates. But walking into Refaat's class, an unmistakable sense of optimism dominated the scene. His infectious energy flowed throughout the classroom and lingered even after he had departed. Refaat breathed life into his students. He sensed in many of us a burning desire for meaningfulness amidst the ubiquitous despair and helplessness. He cultivated our passion for words and for composition. He opened new horizons for us, new possibilities for resistance, for discursivity, for turning words into weapons, for being relevant, for fighting meaningfully, for harnessing the power of narration. We were bound together through our devotion to our people, our love of our homeland, our conviction in the justness of our struggle, our belief in ourselves, and in the goodness and the universality of our humanity.

I had the privilege to be Refaat's student and to interact with him closely. I learned immeasurably from Refaat in and outside the classroom. I went on to complete my postgraduate studies and doctoral research in England and Australia and chose to pursue academic research in sociology and political theory having first been exposed to the ideas that formed the foundation of my work in Refaat's classes during my undergraduate years in Gaza. Never once had I lost sight of what I hoped to achieve in my work, and that is to be a relevant fighter: to turn words into weapons, and to harness the power of narration. This is Refaat's legacy that lives in us, his students, his family, his friends, and his people. Yet, Refaat's legacy cannot be captured in words. For he was a man whose life was composed of words, of stories, of poems, of narratives, and of compositions. Indeed, words cannot do justice to the man whose weapon against oppression was words. Refaat was murdered. He was allowed to be murdered. But Refaat did not die. For Refaat cannot die.

Rawan Yaghi

2013

Rawan Yaghi is a twenty-year-old Palestinian from Gaza. Rawan started as an English Literature student at the Islamic University of Gaza, then transferred to the University of Oxford in the United Kingdom. In addition to writing, Rawan also likes to draw. She started writing in English after the 2008–9 offensive on Gaza. In her narratives, Rawan mainly chooses children's points of views, because she feels their voices are often more powerful in conveying Gazans' plight and hopes. Rawan's stories are drawn from real stories that take place every time an Israeli plane drops heavy bombs, because every time there is an attack there is a child who gets trapped under rubble. Every time a pilot, following orders, presses his or her button to direct a high-tech rocket, a child is traumatized, another is killed, a third is left lonely, and another is turned into a disfigured pound of flesh.

Rawan writes to tell the stories of these children because she does not want to see them go through more pain. When people feel their pain, efforts can be done to stop it. Rawan longs for freedom, as much of a cliché as this sounds. Born as a refugee and feeling displaced ever since she could remember, she has missed a land and a feeling that she has never been allowed to have or experience.

In her own words: *I believe in literature's power to cross borders and walls. I have experienced fiction's ability to erase mental boundaries of nationalities and prejudices, and its ability to reach the human core of people, so I hope my works will make others feel the same experience.*

Sometimes, I feel I own something through my writings. I experience a sort of freedom that I allow myself to have and which I have the ability to allow no one else to violate. And although my writings are surrounded by walls and are set in wars, they make me feel free, because I choose to write them, refusing to keep silent.

2024

He was thin and took long strides when he walked. When his head wasn't absorbed in a book, he held it high, often making a joke or listening intently to the person he's speaking to. He always elbowed a book, close to his ribs. I've known Refaat half of my life.

I had first heard about him from my sister whom he taught at the Islamic University of Gaza. She was part of an online forum he created for his students to talk about their courses, submit work, discuss creative ideas, and write. I joined this forum when I was 14 and that's where I learned my first Orwell reference and first got to know Refaat.

Later, Refaat taught me as part of a US-funded two-year scholarship for excelling 14–16 year old students. I remember my classmates were loyal to our previous teacher but five minutes after Refaat walked into our class, he had our full attention. We were hungry for a teacher like him. He challenged us, overloaded us with information, listened to our nonsense. I wrote my first story in English and published it on his forum. The story was about a child who loses his best friend but having struggled with crying his whole life, he goes home and stares at the ceiling all night. I remember Refaat immediately taking me in, encouraging me from day one to write more. He saw me and lifted me up.

After I finished high school, I was torn between doing an engineering degree or an English Literature degree. He encouraged me to do the latter. It helped that he was a professor at the IUG program. It was at IUG and under Refaat's guidance that I was introduced to Italian literature, reading Pirandello and going back to Dante and Petrarch. I carried this knowledge into my degree at the University of Oxford, which he of course also encouraged me to apply for. He taught us English Literature in the context of world literature. He built the short story class model to reflect his philosophy, drawing on the works of Ghassan Kanafani, Virginia Woolf, Chekhov, Hemingway, and Pirandello. He stressed the universality of literature, its ability to knock down prejudices and challenge power. He believed in it. He was killed because of his work and because of the prejudices he fought and the powers he challenged.

I can't box Refaat into a memory or two. Refaat was part of me. When I lost him, I cried. I screamed. He loved what he did and he loved his students who usually became his friends. We loved him. He was taken from us.

Acknowledgments

The input many people put into this book is deeply appreciated. I would like to thank Helena Cobban, Kimberly MacVaugh, and the rest of the team at Just World Books for making this book a reality. A thank-you is due to Annie Robbins for her support of many of the promising writers. Yousef Aljamal, a contributor to this book, also helped with the logistics at the Center for Political and Development Studies in Gaza City and Samiha Olwan did a great job reading texts. Two people have done this book the best favor: Sarah Ali, herself a contributor to the book and who was there from day one, suggested texts, read them, and worked with me and the writers to give the stories the form and shape they now have; and Diana Ghazzawi of Wordreams Editing and Design, whose sharp eye and editing skills polished the stories.